NOTHING

JANNE TELLER

TRANSLATED FROM THE
DANISH BY MARTIN AITKEN

WWW.STRIDENTPUBLISHING.CO.UK

Published by
Strident Publishing Ltd
22 Strathwhillan Drive
The Orchard, Hairmyres
East Kilbride G75 8GT

Tel: +44 (0)1355 220588
info@stridentpublishing.co.uk
www.stridentpublishing.co.uk

Originally published in Denmark in 2000 as Intet
by Dansklærerforeningens Forlag A/S.

A catalogue record for this book is
available from the British Library.

ISBN: 9781905537327

The publisher acknowledges subsidy from the Scottish
Arts Council towards the publication of this volume.

Printed and bound by CPI Group (UK) Ltd.

TRANSLATOR'S NOTE I

Tæring is a fictional place. Its name is derived from a verb meaning to gradually consume, corrode, or eat through, for example in the way rust may eat through metal. Keeping its name in the English translation means losing this immediate association, yet allows the reader an important sense of being somewhere foreign.

I

Nothing matters.
I have known that for a long time.
So nothing is worth doing.
I just realized that.

II

Pierre Anthon left school the day he realized that nothing was worth doing because nothing meant anything anyway.

The rest of us stayed on.

And although the teachers had a job on their hands tidying up after Pierre Anthon in the class-room as well as in our heads, part of Pierre Anthon remained stuck inside of us. Maybe that was why it all turned out the way it did.

It was the second week of August. The sun was heavy, making us slow and irritable, the tarmac caught on the soles of our sneakers, and apples and pears were just ripe enough to lie snugly in the hand, the perfect missiles. We looked neither left nor right. It was the first day of school after summer holiday. The classroom smelled of detergent and weeks of emptiness, the windows reflected clear and bright, and the blackboard was yet to be blanketed with chalk dust. The desks stood two by two in rows as straight as hospital corridors, as they did only on this one day of the year. Class 7A.

We found our seats without caring to shake any familiarity into the orderliness.

There's a time for everything. Better things, jumbled things. But not today!

Mr. Eskildsen bid us welcome with the same joke he made every year.

"Take joy in this day," he said. "There would be no such thing as vacation, were it not for such a thing as school."

We laughed. Not because it was funny, but because him saying it was.

It was then that Pierre Anthon stood up.

"Nothing matters," he announced. "I've known that for a long time. So nothing's worth doing. I just realized that." Calm and collected, he bent down and put everything he had just taken out back into his bag. He nodded goodbye with a disinterested look and left the classroom without closing the door behind him.

The door smiled. It was the first time I'd seen it do that. Pierre Anthon left the door ajar like a grinning abyss that would swallow me up into the outside with him if only I let myself go. Smiling at whom? At me, at us. I looked around the class. The uncomfortable silence told me the others had felt it too.

We were supposed to amount to something.

Something was the same as someone, and even if nobody ever said so out loud, it was hardly left unspoken either. It was just in the air, or in the time, or in the fence surrounding the school, or in our pillows, or in the soft toys that after having served us so loyally had now been unjustly discarded and left to gather dust in attics or basements. I hadn't known. Pierre Anthon's smiling door told me. I still didn't know with my mind, but all the same I knew.

All of a sudden I was scared. Scared of Pierre Anthon.

Scared, more scared, most scared.

We lived in Tæring, an outpost to a fair-sized provincial town. Not swank, but almost. We'd often be reminded of the fact. Nobody ever said so out loud, yet it was hardly left unspoken either. Neat, yellow-washed brick homes and red bungalows with gardens running all the way round, new grey-brown rows with gardens out front, and then the apartment houses, home to those we never played with. There were some old timber-framed cottages, too, and farms that were no longer farms, the land sold off for development, and a few rather more imposing whitewashed residences for those who were more almost-swank than the rest of us.

Tæring School was situated on the corner of two streets. All of us except Elise lived down the one called Tæringvej. Sometimes Elise would go the long way around just to walk to school with the rest of us. At least until Pierre Anthon left.

Pierre Anthon lived with his father and the rest of the commune in an old farmhouse at Tæringvej number 25. Pierre Anthon's father and the commune were all hippies who were still stuck in '68. That was what our parents said, and even though we didn't really know what it meant, we said it too. In the front yard by the street there was a plum tree. It was a tall tree, old and crooked, leaning out over the hedge to tempt us with its dusty red Victoria plums which none of us could reach. Other years we'd jump to get at the plums. We stopped doing that. Pierre Anthon left school to sit in the plum tree and pelt us with unripe plums. Some of them hit home. Not because Pierre Anthon was aiming at us, because that wasn't worth it, he proclaimed. It was just chance that made it so.

He yelled at us too.

"It's all a waste of time," he yelled one day. "Everything begins only to end. The moment you were born you began to die. That's how it is with everything."

"The Earth is four billion, six hundred million years old, and you're going to reach one hundred at the most!" he yelled another day. "It's not even worth the bother."

And he went on:

"It's all a big masquerade, all make-believe and making out you're the best at it."

Nothing had ever indicated that Pierre Anthon was the smartest among us, but suddenly we all knew he was. He was onto something. Even if none of us cared to admit it. Not to our parents, not to our teachers, not to each other. Not even to ourselves. We didn't want to live in the world Pierre Anthon was telling us about. We were going to amount to something, be someone.

The smiling door wasn't going to lure us.

No, sir. No way!

That was why we came up with the idea. "We" is perhaps an exaggeration, because it was Pierre Anthon who got us going.

It was one morning when Sofie had been hit in the head by two hard plums one after another, and she was so mad at Pierre Anthon for just sitting there in his tree, disheartening all of us.

"All you ever do is sit there gawking. Is that any

better?" she yelled.

"I'm not gawking," Pierre Anthon replied calmly. "I'm contemplating the sky and getting used to doing nothing."

"The heck you are!" Sofie yelled angrily and hurled a stick up at Pierre Anthon in the plum tree. It landed in the hedge, way beneath him.

Pierre Anthon laughed and hollered so loud they could have heard him all the way up at the school.

"If something's worth getting upset about, then there must be something worth getting happy about. And if something's worth getting happy about, then there must be something that matters. But there isn't!" He raised his voice a notch and roared: "In a few years you'll all be dead and forgotten and diddly squat, nothing, so you might just as well start getting used to it!"

That was when we understood we had to get Pierre Anthon out of that plum tree.

III

A plum tree has many branches.
So many, endless branches.
All too many endless branches.

Tæring School was large and square and grey as
concrete. It was in two storeys and in essence an
ugly building, but few of us ever had time to think
about that, and certainly not now that we were
spending all our time not thinking about what
Pierre Anthon was saying.

Yet this particular Tuesday morning, eight days
into the new school year, it was as though the ugli-
ness of the school struck us like a whole fistful of
Pierre Anthon's bitter plums.

I walked with Jon-Johan and Sofie through the gate into the schoolyard and just behind us came Ursula-Marie and Gerda, and we all fell quite silent as we turned the corner and saw the school building. I can't explain how, but it was like it was something Pierre Anthon was making us see. As if the nothing he kept yelling about up in the plum tree had overtaken us on the way and got here first.

The school was so grey and ugly and angular that I almost couldn't catch my breath, and all of a sudden it was as if the school was life itself, and it wasn't how life was supposed to look but did anyway. I felt a violent urge to run over to Tæringvej 25 and climb up to Pierre Anthon in his plum tree and stare into the sky until I became a part of the outside and nothing and never had to think about anything again. But I was supposed to amount to something, be someone, so I stayed where I was and just looked the other way and dug my nails into the palm of my hand until it hurt good and strong.

Smiling door—Open! Close!

I wasn't the only one to feel outside calling.

"We have to do something," Jon-Johan whispered, making sure the others just ahead of us didn't hear him. Jon-Johan could play the guitar and sing Beatles songs so you could hardly tell the difference between him and the real ones.

"He's right!" whispered Ursula-Marie, whom I suspected of having a crush on Jon-Johan, and sure enough Gerda sniggered right away and stabbed the air with her elbow, Ursula-Marie having walked on in the meantime.

"But what?" I whispered, breaking into a trot. The kids from the other class had come disconcertingly close, among them the bully boys who twanged rubber bands and dried peas at the girls whenever the opportunity arose, and my opportunity looked like it was going to arise pretty soon.

Jon-Johan sent a note round in maths, and the whole class met down on the football field after school. All of us except Henrik, because Henrik was the son of our biology teacher, and we didn't want to run any kind of risk.

To begin with it felt like an age we were just standing there talking about other things and making
out we weren't all thinking about one and the
same thing. At last, Jon-Johan drew himself up
and declared almost solemnly that we all had to
pay attention.

"It can't go on like this," his speech began, and
that was how he ended it too, after briefly stating
what we all of us knew, that we couldn't go on
making like things mattered as long as Pierre Anthon remained in his plum tree, yelling at us that
nothing mattered.

We had just started seventh grade, and we were
all so modern and well-versed in life and being
in the world that we knew that everything was
more about how it appeared than how it was. The
most important thing, in any circumstance, was
to amount to something that really looked like it
was something. And though that something as yet
seemed rather vague and unclear to us, it certainly
had nothing to do with sitting in a plum tree pitching plums into the street.

If Pierre Anthon thought he could make us think

any different he had another thing coming.

"He's bound to climb down when winter comes and there are no more plums," said Pretty Rosa.

It didn't help.

For one thing, the sun was still blazing away in the sky, and winter looked like it was a long way off. For another, there was no reason to believe that Pierre Anthon couldn't stay in his plum tree winter or not, even if there were no plums. All he had to do was dress warmly.

"You're going to have to beat up on him, then." It was the boys I was talking to, for even though we girls could scratch some, it was obvious that it was the boys who would have to bear the brunt.

They looked around at each other.

They didn't think it was a good idea. Pierre Anthon was solid and thickset, with a splash of freckles on the nose he'd broken two years ago when he'd butted some kid from four years above us down in the town. Despite his broken nose, Pierre Anthon had won the fight. The other kid had been sent to hospital with concussion.

"Fighting's not a good idea," said Jon-Johan,

and the other boys nodded, ending the discussion there and then, even though we girls probably lost some degree of respect for them on that occasion.

"We should pray to God," suggested Holy Karl, whose father was something big in the Inner Mission, his mother as well, for that matter.

"Shut up, Karl!" Otto hissed. He pinched Holy Karl until Holy Karl couldn't possibly shut up, but squealed like a hog with its head in a fire, and the rest of us had to get Otto to lay off so that all his squealing didn't attract the caretaker.

"We could make a complaint about him," suggested Little Ingrid, who was so small we didn't always remember she was there. Today, though, we remembered, and responded all at once:

"Who to?"

"To Mr Eskildsen." Little Ingrid noted our astonished expressions. Eskildsen was our registration teacher, and Eskildsen wore a black raincoat and a gold watch and didn't care to deal with problems on any scale. "To the Principal, then," she went on.

"The Principal!" Otto spluttered, and would have pinched Little Ingrid if Jon-Johan hadn't quickly stepped in between them.

"We can't complain to Eskildsen or to the Principal or to any other grown-up, because if we complain about Pierre Anthon sitting in his plum tree, we'll have to tell them why we're complaining. And then we'll have to tell them what Pierre Anthon's saying. Which we can't, because the grown-ups won't want to hear that we know that nothing matters and that everybody is just making like it does." Jon-Johan threw up his arms, and we imagined all the experts, the educators and psychologists who would come and observe us and talk to us and reason with us until eventually we would give in and again start pretending that things really did matter. Jon-Johan was right: it was a waste of time that would get us nowhere.

For a while no-one said anything. I screwed my eyes up at the sun, then stared at the white football goals without their nets, then behind me at the shot-putt circle, the high-jump mattresses and the running track. A gentle breeze was blowing through the beech hedge that ran round the football field and suddenly it was all like a gym lesson and a day like any other, and I almost forgot why we had to get Pierre Anthon out of his plum tree. "For all I care he can sit up there and yell till he rots," I thought to myself. I said nothing. The thought was true only at the moment it was thought.

"Let's pelt him with stones," Otto suggested, and now came a lengthy discussion about where to get hold of the stones and how big they should be and who was going to throw them, for the idea was good.

Good, better, best.

It was the only one we had.

IV

One stone, two stones, many stones.

They were all piled up in the bike trailer Holy Karl used every Tuesday afternoon for delivering the local paper and the church newsletter the first Wednesday of the month. We'd gathered them down by the stream where they were big and round, and the trailer was heavy as a dead horse.

We were all going to throw.

"Two each at least," Jon-Johan commanded.

Otto kept tally to make sure we each took our turn. Even Henrik, the little butter-up, had been summoned and duly delivered his two shots, neither of which came even close. Maiken's and Sofie's were marginally better.

"So nothing's got you all scared then?" Pierre Anthon hollered as he followed Ursula-Maries's pathetic shots and watched them land in the hedge.

"You're only up there because your dad's still stuck in 68!" shouted Huge Hans, and hurled a stone into the tree. It smacked into a plum that splattered in all directions.

We hooted.

I hooted with the rest of them, even though I knew neither claim was true. Pierre Anthon's father and the rest of the commune grew organic vegetables and practised exotic religions and were receptive to the spiritual world, alternative treatments, and their fellow human beings. But that wasn't the reason it wasn't true. It wasn't true because Pierre Anthon's father wore a buzz cut and worked for a computer company, and the whole thing was up-to-the-minute and had nothing to do with either 68 or Pierre Anthon in the slightest.

"My dad's not stuck in anything, and neither am I!" Pierre Anthon yelled, wiping splatterings of plum from his arm. "I'm sat here in nothing. And better to be sitting in nothing than in something that isn't anything!"

It was early morning.

The sun was beating down from the east, directly into Pierre Anthon's eyes. He had to shield them with his hand if he wanted to see us. We were standing with our backs to the sun around the trailer on the opposite side of the road. Out of range of Pierre Anthon's plums.

We didn't answer him.

It was Richard's turn. And Richard hurled a stone that cracked hard against the trunk of the plum tree, and another that tore in among the leaves and plums and just missed Pierre Anthon's left ear. Then it was my turn. I've never been good at throwing, but I was angry and determined, and though my first shot ended up in the hedge next to Ursula-Marie's, the second rattled right into the branch on which Pierre Anthon was sitting.

"Hey, Agnes," Pierre Anthon shouted down at me. "You're having such problems believing things matter?"

I flung a third stone, and this time I must have grazed him because we heard a howl, and for a moment it was quiet up in the tree. Then Otto threw, but too high and too far, and Pierre Anthon began his hollering again.

"If you live to be eighty, you'll have slept thirty years away, gone to school and sat with homework for nine, and worked for almost fourteen. Since you've already spent more than six years being little kids and playing, and you're later going to be spending at least twelve cleaning a house, cooking food and looking after your own kids, it means you've got nine years at most to live." Pierre Anthon tossed a plum into the air. It followed a gentle arc before plunging into the gutter. "And you want to spend those nine years pretending you've amounted to something in a masquerade that means nothing, when instead you could start enjoying your nine years right away." He pulled another plum off a branch, reclined contentedly in the fork of the tree and appeared to be weighing the plum in his hand. He took a big bite and laughed. The Victorias were ripening.

"It's not a masquerade!" Otto yelled, threatening Pierre Anthon with a fist.

"It's not a masquerade!" Huge Hans joined in and launched another stone.

"Then how come everyone's making like everything that isn't important is very important, all the while they're so busy pretending what's really important isn't important at all?" Pierre Anthon laughed and drew an arm across his face to wipe away the plum juice from his chin. "How come it's so important we learn to say please and thank you and the same to you and how do you do when soon none of us will be doing anything any more and everybody knows that instead they could be sitting here eating plums, watching the world go by and getting used to being a part of nothing?"

Holy Karl's two stones were sent off in quick succession.

"If nothing matters, then it's better doing nothing than something. Especially if something is throwing stones because you haven't the guts to climb trees."

The stones rained in on the plum tree from all sides. The pitching order was forgotten. Everyone was throwing at once now, and soon Pierre Anthon let out a howl and fell out of the tree, landing with a thump on the grass behind the hedge. Which was just as well because all our stones were used up and time was getting on. Holy Karl had to be off home with his trailer if he was going to make it to school before the bell.

The next morning it was quiet in the plum tree when we passed by on our way to school.

Otto was the first one to cross the street. Then followed Huge Hans, who jumped up heavily and yanked away two Victorias with a handful of leaves and a holler, and when there was still no reaction the rest of us followed, jubilant.

We'd won!

Victory is sweet. Victory is. Victory.

Two days later Pierre Anthon was back in his plum tree with a Band-Aid across his forehead and a whole new range of repartee:

"Even if you learn something and think you're

good at it, there'll always be someone who's better."

"Pipe down!" I yelled back. "I'm going to be
something worth being! And famous, too!"

"Sure you are, Agnes." Pierre Anthon's voice
was kind, almost pitying. "You'll be a fashion
designer and teeter around in high heels and
make like you're really something and make others think they are too as long as they're wearing
your label." He shook his head. "But you'll find
out you're a clown in a trivial circus where everyone tries to convince each other how vital it is
to have a certain look one year and another the
next. And then you'll find out that fame and the
big wide world are outside of you, and that inside there's nothing, and always will be, no matter what you do."

I surveyed the ground; there were no stones
anywhere.

"Shut up!" I screamed, but Pierre Anthon kept on.

"Why not admit from the outset that nothing
matters and just enjoy the nothing that is?"

I gave him the finger.

Pierre Anthon just laughed.

Furious, I grabbed Ursula Marie by the arm, because Ursula-Marie was my friend with blue hair and six thick braids, and that was definitely something. Blue, bluer, bluest. If my mother hadn't expressly forbidden it, my hair would have been blue, too. As it was, I had to make do with the six braids, which weren't particularly impressive given my fine, wispy hair, but at least it was something.

Only a few days passed before Jon-Johan again summoned us to the football field.

There were no good suggestions, but loads of poor ones. None of us was listening to Otto any more, and if he hadn't been the strongest in the class, at least since Pierre Anthon had left school, we would all have laid into him.

Just as we were about to break up and leave, not being able to come up with anything anyway, Sofie stepped forward.

"We have to prove to Pierre Anthon that something matters," was all she said. Yet it was plenty, for we all knew right away what it was we had to do.

We set out the very next day.

V

Sofie lived at exactly the point where Tæring stopped being town and became countryside. Behind the yellow-washed house where Sofie lived with her parents was a large field with an abandoned sawmill at one end. The sawmill wasn't used for anything anymore and was to be torn down to make room for a recreation facility the town dignitaries had been talking about for years. Even so, nobody was really counting on that recreation facility, and although the sawmill had gradually fallen into disrepair, with broken windows and holes in the roof, it was still there and was exactly what we needed.

At lunch recess we all handed over our one and two and five kroner coins to Jon-Johan, who ran the entire way to the hardware store, made our purchase and ran all the way back again clutching a brand-new combination padlock.

There was some discussion about what code to choose, since everyone thought their own birthday provided the most suitable combination of figures. Eventually we agreed on the fifth of February, it being the day of Pierre Anthon's birth. Five-zero-two were the numbers we all concentrated on committing to memory, so much so that we forgot about our homework and about paying attention in class, and Mr. Eskildsen started growing suspicious and asked if our heads were full of sparrows or whether we'd just lost whatever little it was that had been attached to our necks.

We didn't reply. Not one of us. Five-zero-two!

We had the sawmill, we had the lock and we knew what we had to do. Nevertheless, it was a lot harder than we had reckoned. With Pierre Anthon being in some way right about nothing mattering, it was no easy thing to start collecting something that did.

Again, it was Sofie who saved the day.

"We just play along with the idea," she said, and gradually we all found our own ploys to help us.

Elise remembered when she was six and had cried when an Alsatian dog had bitten the head off her doll, so she dug out the old doll and its chewed-off head from the boxes in her basement and brought them along with her to the sawmill. Holy Karl brought an old hymnbook that was missing its front and back and quite a number of its hymns, but which nevertheless ran with no other defects from page 27 to page 389. Ursula-Marie delivered a pink ivory comb missing two teeth, and Jon-Johan chipped in with a Beatles tape that had lost all sound, but that he had never had the heart to throw out.

Others went from house to house asking if they could have anything that meant something. One or two doors were slammed in our faces, but we were also given the most wondrous things. The old folks were the best. They gave us china dogs that could nod their heads and which were only slightly chipped, photographs of parents long since dead, or the toys of children long since departed into adulthood. We were given clothes that had been treasured and worn to threads, and even a single rose from a bridal bouquet thirty-six years old.

The rose, however, made us girls somewhat faint-hearted, because it really was something we felt mattered, the white bridal dream with the wedding bouquet and the kiss from the man who was to be ours for ever. But then Laura said that the lady who had given it to us had divorced only five years on. And since many of our own parents were also divorced, if indeed they had ever been married at all, that dream clearly wasn't worth our time.

The heap grew and grew.

In just a few days it grew almost as tall as Little Ingrid. Nevertheless, it was still short on meaning. We all knew that none of what we had collected really mattered to us – not really - so how were we supposed to convince Pierre Anthon that it did?

He was going to see right through us.

Squat. Zilch. Nothing.

Again, Jon-Johan called us together, and it wasn't long before we had to admit that certain things did matter to us, even if it wasn't much and even if they weren't all that important. Still, it was a better take than the one we had.

Dennis was the first. He brought a whole stack of Dungeons & Dragons books he had read over and over and almost learned off by heart. Otto, however, soon discovered that four of the series were missing, and said that Dennis was going to have to give them up, too.

Dennis blew up and told Otto to mind his own business, that we all knew that wasn't part of the scheme, and we were so mean, all of us. But the more Dennis yelled, the more the rest of us maintained that the books plainly mattered a whole lot to him. And hadn't we just agreed that it was the things that meant most to us that had to go on the heap if it was ever going to convince Pierre Anthon to climb out of his tree?

When Dennis had first handed over the last four of his Dungeons & Dragons books, it was as if the meaning started to take off. Dennis knew how fond Sebastian was of his fishing rod. And Sebastian knew that Richard had a thing about his black football. And Richard had noticed how Laura always wore the same African parrot earrings.

We should have stopped even before it got this far. Now it was somehow too late, even though I did what I could.

"This isn't going to work," I said.

"Ha!" Gerda scoffed, and she was pointing at my green wedge sandals I'd spent all summer persuading my mom to buy me, and that she'd only just bought me recently for half-price in the sales.

I knew it was going to come. And to be honest, that was probably why I tried to stop the whole affair. It would only be a matter of time before someone got around to my sandals. The fact that it was Giggling Gerda, little bye-baby-bumpkin, only made things worse. At first I tried to pass it off, as if I hadn't even noticed what it was she was pointing at, but Laura wasn't letting me off the hook.

"The sandals, Agnes," she said, and there was no way out.

I squatted down and was about to untie them, but then I couldn't get myself to do it and stood up again.

"I can't," I said. "My mom's going to ask where they are, and then the grown-ups are going to figure the whole thing out." I thought I was smart. But I wasn't.

"You think you're any better than the rest of us?" cried Sebastian. "What do you suppose my dad's going to think I've done with my fishing rod?" As if to underline his words, he grabbed hold of the line and fishhook that dangled from the heap.

"And what have I done with my books?"

"And where's my football?"

"And my earrings?"

I'd lost and I knew it. All I could do was ask for a few days' respite.

"Just until summer's over."

There was no mercy. Even if they did let me borrow a pair of sneakers from Sofie, so I wouldn't have to walk home barefoot.

Sofie's sneakers were too small, they pinched at my big toe, and the way home from the sawmill was a whole lot longer than usual. I was crying as I turned into the street and walked the last part of the way up to the house alone.

I didn't go in, but sat down in the bike shed where I could be seen neither from the street nor the house. I pulled Sofie's sneakers off my feet and kicked them into a corner. The image of my green wedge sandals on top of the heap of meaning wouldn't go away.

I looked down at my bare feet and decided Gerda
was going to pay.

VI

It took me three days to find Gerda's weak spot, and during those three days I was sweetness itself with her.

I had never liked Gerda. She had a way of spitting when she spoke, even more when she giggled, which she did almost all the time. Besides that, she would never let Ursula-Marie alone, and Ursula-Marie was my best friend and so very special, not only because she had blue hair and six braids, but also because she only ever wore black. If my mom hadn't kept on sabotaging it all by buying those garish clothes for me, I would have worn only black too. As it was, I had to make do with one pair of black trousers, two black T-shirts with funny

.

37

slogans and one black woollen undershirt that was still too warm to wear yet at the beginning of September.

But now it was all about Gerda.

I swapped hair elastics with Gerda, whispered with her about boys, and confided to her that I had warmed a bit to Huge Hans (which wasn't true in the slightest, but though you're not supposed to lie, this was what my older brother referred to as *force masheure*, and even though I wasn't quite sure what it meant, it definitely entailed that right now lying was okay).

The first two days didn't yield much. Gerda didn't seem to be especially fond of anything. Or perhaps she had seen through me. There were some old paper dolls her grandmother had given her, but I knew she hadn't played with them for several years. At one point she showed me a picture of her favourite movie star, who she was swooning over and kissed every night before going to bed. Then there was a whole stack of romantic novels with doctors kissing nurses and living happily ever after. I admit I occasionally wouldn't have minded borrowing them, and Gerda would probably have stifled a tear or two had she been made to hand them over, but it was still just trifles, nothing that truly mattered. Then on the third day I found it.

It was while we were sitting in Gerda's room drinking mugs of tea and listening to a tape her father had just given her that I discovered Gerda's weak spot. We'd spent the two previous days at Gerda's mother's place, in the room she had there. It was filled with girls' stuff, all sequins and tinsel. Now we were sat in her room at her father's place where she stayed every other week. It wasn't the stereo tape-deck or the inflatable plastic armchair or the idol posters on the walls that made this room different from the one at her mother's place, for she had a stereo tape-deck and an inflatable plastic armchair and idol posters on the walls there, too. No, the thing that made the room at Gerda's father's place special was that in the corner stood a very large cage with a very small hamster inside.

The hamster's name was Oscarlittle, and Oscarlittle was what I declared the next day that Gerda had to give up to the heap of meaning.

Gerda wept and said she was going to snitch about me and Huge Hans. I howled laughing when I told her it was just something I'd made up on account of *force masheure*. That made Gerda cry even more and say I was the cruelest of anyone she knew. And when she had cried for two hours and was still inconsolable, I started having second thoughts, thinking maybe she was right. But then I saw my green wedge sandals on top of the heap and wouldn't budge.

Ursula-Marie and I walked Gerda home to get Oscarlittle right away. We weren't giving her any chance to get out of it.

Gerda's father lived in one of the new row houses. They were grey-brown and built in brick - at least the outer layer was, around the concrete - and all the rooms were fitted with large, easy-to-open windows. The row houses lay at the other end of Tæring, where until recently there had been meadows full of grey-brown sheep. The fact that the house was at the opposite end of Tæring made the walk long and exhausting, but the main thing was the large windows. Gerda's father was home, and Oscarlittle had to be smuggled out. Ursula-Marie went with Gerda into her room, while I stood outside ready to receive. Oscarlittle was handed through the window and I stuffed him inside an old rusty cage we had dug out for the purpose. Gerda herself just stood sniveling in a corner of the room and refused to lend a hand.

"Shut up, Gerda!" I snapped eventually, unable to take any more of her whining. "Or there's a dead hamster going on the heap!"

It didn't make Gerda stop sniveling, but it did quieten her down enough to make things tolerable again and to allow her to leave the house without her father catching on.

Oscarlittle was mottled white and brown and actually fairly cute with his trembling whiskers, and I was happy not to have to do away with him. The cage, on the other hand, was heavy and unwieldy, and the road to the sawmill unendingly long. We should have borrowed Holy Karl's trailer. We hadn't, so we took turns carrying. Gerda too. There was no reason for her not to take her fair share of the aching shoulders Ursula-Marie and I were getting. It took an age to reach the field and the sawmill, and Oscarlittle squeaked the entire way as if I really was going to kill him, but eventually we got there and could put the cage with Oscarlittle down in the half-light inside the door.

We let Gerda line the cage with some old sawdust, and after she had given Oscarlittle an extra portion of hamster food and a bowl of fresh water I climbed up the stepladder and placed him and the cage on top of the heap.

I climbed down again, dragged the ladder away and stood to admire the heap with the cage like a star slightly crooked on top. Then I noticed how quiet it was in the mill.

Quiet. Quieter. All quiet.

It was so quiet I suddenly couldn't help but notice how big and empty the place was, how many cracks and crevices there were in the concrete floor that could just be picked out beneath the dirt of the sawdust, how thick the cobwebs were that clung to every beam and joist, how many holes there were in the roof, and how few window panes were still intact. I surveyed the surroundings from one end of the mill to the other, up and down, down and up, then finally turned my gaze to my classmates.

They were still staring silently at the cage.

It was as though Oscarlittle had added something to the heap of meaning that neither my green wedge sandals, nor Sebastian's fishing rod, nor Richard's football had been able to. I was pretty pleased with myself for having come up with the idea, so it stung that the others seemed less than enthusiastic.

It was Otto who came to my rescue.

"Now, *there's* something that's got meaning!" he exclaimed, looking away from Oscarlittle and toward me.

"Pierre Anthon's never going to top that," Huge Hans added, and no-one seemed to be protesting.

I had to bite my tongue not to blush from pride.

It was getting late, and most of us had to be getting off home for supper. We took a final admiring look at our bulging heap, then Sofie turned off the lights and closed the door behind us. Jon-Johan put the padlock on and we hurried away in all directions.

It was Gerda's turn.

VII

Gerda wasn't particularly inventive and said only that Maiken was to hand over her telescope. We all knew Maiken had invested two years and all her savings in her telescope, and that she spent every evening, when the sky was clear, observing the stars, for she was going to be an astrophysicist. Even so, it was a disappointing choice.

Maiken herself, though, proved more adventurous.

Without needing time to think about it, she looked directly at Frederik and said:

"The Dannebrog."

It was like Frederik started to shrink, he grew thinner and smaller and more and more red in the face and began to shake his head vigorously.

Frederik had brown hair and brown eyes and was always dressed in a white shirt and blue pants with creases the other boys did their best to ruin. And like his parents, who were married and not divorced and never would be, Frederik believed in Denmark and the Royal House and was forbidden to ever play with Hussain.

The Dannebrog, our proud flag, had descended from the skies in twelve-hundred-and-something, Frederik maintained, in order that the Danish king could prevail over the enemy in Latvia. What the Danish king was doing in Latvia, Frederik was unable to enlighten us with, and nor would it have helped him any had he known.

We definitely couldn't have cared less about kings or Latvia as we hooted:

"Dannebrog, Dannebrog. Frederik fetch your Dannebrog!"

As songs go it was hardly noteworthy, but we repeated it over and over to our great amusement. What amused us most though was probably the horrified expression on Frederik's face.

In the front yard of the red bungalow where
Frederik lived with his married and undivorced
parents stood Tæring's tallest flagpole. From that
flagpole the Dannebrog waved from sunrise to sun-
set every single Sunday, as well as on just about
any special occasion, whether it were the Queen's
birthday or Frederik's, or just a regular holiday.
In Frederik's family running up the flag was the
man's duty and privilege, and since Frederik had
recently celebrated his fourteenth birthday he had
proudly accepted taking on both the duty and the
privilege from his father.

It went without saying that Frederik had no intention of giving up the flag. But we were unyielding and pitiless, and the following day the Dannebrog took its place on the heap of meaning.

We sang the national anthem and stood to attention
while Frederik fastened the red and white emblem
to the iron rod Jon-Johan had found at the back of
the mill and which was now planted firmly in the
middle of the heap.

The Dannebrog was a lot bigger up close than when waving at the top of its flagpole, and I felt slightly uneasy about the whole venture, considering the history and the nation and all. It didn't seem to bother any of the others, though, and when I thought of the meaning I knew that Maiken had hit home: with the Dannebrog on high, the heap of meaning sure looked a whole lot like something.

Something. Lots. Meaning!

That Frederik had a wicked streak was an idea that would never have occurred to any of us. Yet he rose significantly in our esteem when he demanded lady William's diary.

Lady William was, how should I put it? Lady William.

And lady William's diary was a very special thing indeed, bound in dark leather and French pulp and with meticulously inscribed pages inside that looked like they were sandwich paper, but were apparently a whole lot finer.

Now Ladylady William huffed and he puffed, and under no circumstances was he willing, and he waved his hands about in a manner we girls later tried to copy as we almost died laughing.

It was to no avail.

The diary was given up to the heap of meaning, though without its key, which Frederik had forgotten to claim, thereby falling just as quickly in our esteem as he had risen.

Lady William declared in a nasal tone and rather condescendingly that with the addition of his diary the heap of meaning had reached an entirely new *plateau*—he took a particular delight in words that came from French and that the rest of us didn't know the meaning of. Whatever it meant, it was because of this plateau that he begged Anna-Li's forgiveness for her now having to give up her certificate of adoption.

Anna-Li was Korean despite being Danish, and of her two sets of parents she had only ever known the Danish ones. Anna-Li never uttered a word and never interfered in anything, she just blinked some and looked down at the ground whenever anyone spoke to her. She wasn't even saying anything now. It was Ursula-Marie who protested.

"That doesn't count, William. A certificate of adoption is like a birth certificate. It's not something you can give away."

"Well, I'm most sorry," lady William retorted with an indulgent air. "My diary is my life. If it may be sacrificed to the heap, then so may a certificate of adoption. Was it not our intention that the heap should be meaningful?"

"Not in that sense," Ursula-Marie replied, shaking her head so her six blue braids flew about the air.

Lady William persisted politely, and we didn't really know how else to object, so we simply stood there, mulling it over.

Then, to our astonishment Anna-Li said a whole lot all at once.

"It doesn't matter," she began. "Or rather, it matters a lot. But that's the whole idea, isn't it? Otherwise the heap of meaning has no meaning at all, and then Pierre Anthon will be right about nothing meaning anything."

Anna-Li was right.

The certificate of adoption was added to the top of the heap, and when Anna-Li declared that Little

Ingrid had to give up her new crutches, nobody objected.

Little Ingrid would have to use her old ones.

The meaning was gathering momentum, and our enthusiasm was boundless when Little Ingrid, quite unperturbed, whispered that Henrik was going to have to bring the snake in formaldehyde.

VIII

In the biology room there were six things worth looking at: the skeleton we called Mr Hansen, the half-man with the detachable organs, a wall poster detailing the female reproductive organs, a dried out and slightly cracked human skull referred to as Hamlet's Handful, a stuffed weasel, and the snake in formaldehyde. Of these, the snake in formaldehyde was by far the most interesting, and Little Ingrid's scheme was for this reason no less than brilliant.

Henrik didn't agree.

Not least because the snake was a cobra that had cost his father a great deal of time, much correspondence and an endless amount of negotiations to secure for the school's collection. Another thing about the snake was that it was disgusting and brought shivers to the spine every time you happened to look at it. With its prehistoric patterns and closely interlocking scales, the body of the snake lay curled in an endless spiral at the bottom of its jar, the head raised keenly, its jagged neck splayed out as though in rage, and as though at any moment the creature was going to discharge its paralyzing venom from between its hissing, flesh-pink jaws.

No-one ever touched the jar voluntarily.

Unless, that is, they could get at least ten kroner for doing so.

Henrik stubbornly and stupidly maintained that the snake in formaldehyde didn't belong on the heap of meaning. However, it helped some that Hussain held the jar with the snake up above Henrik's head at recess (Otto was paying the ten kroner) and threatened to smash it against his skull if Henrik didn't give the snake up to the heap.

The rest of us were just as impatient, insistent that it be done right away. We needed to get finished so we could shut Pierre Anthon up once and for all. The plums were well ripened now, and Pierre Anthon was spitting sticky plum stones at us all the while he was hollering his stuff.

"How come you girls want to be dating?" he'd shouted that same morning as I passed by Tæringvej 25, arm in arm with Ursula-Marie. "First you fall in love, then you start dating, then you fall out of love, and then you split up again."

"Shut it, Pierre Anthon!" Ursula-Marie hollered back at the top of her lungs.

Maybe she felt especially stung, because we'd just been talking about Jon-Johan and this matter of the feelings that we just didn't seem to be able to rein in or fathom.

Pierre Anthon laughed and went on in a more gentle tone:

"And that's the way it goes, time and time over, right until you grow so tired of all that repetition you just decide to make like the one who happens to be closest by is the one and only. What a waste of effort!"

"Just shut up, will you!" I yelled, and started running. Although I wasn't dating, and had no idea who I'd pick if I had to choose there and then, I certainly wanted to, and soon. There was no way I was going to let Pierre Anthon ruin love for me before it even got started.

Ursula-Marie and I ran the entire rest of the way to school, in a mood worse than we could ever recall being in at one and the same time. It didn't even cheer us up when Pretty Rosa reminded us that Pierre Anthon had once dated Sofie for a fortnight and that they had even kissed before it ended again, and that Sofie had then gone on to date Sebastian, while Pierre Anthon had got together with Laura.

That was a story that sounded a bit too much like something I didn't want to hear. And maybe a bit too much like what Pierre Anthon himself had said.

I don't know exactly when it was that Henrik saw his chance to snatch the snake from the biology room, or how he managed to get it to the sawmill without being seen. I only know that Dennis and Richard helped him and that the snake rolled disgustingly like it was alive when they lifted up the jar and placed it on top of the heap.

Oscarlittle didn't like it much either.

The hamster squealed pathetically and cowered in the far corner of its cage, and Gerda cried and told them to wrap newspaper around the snake so we didn't all have to see.

But Oscarlittle's squealing made the snake in formaldehyde even more meaningful, and none of us would agree to have it be packed away.

Instead we turned our gaze expectantly to Henrik.

IX

Henrik was a real butter-up.

He asked for Otto's boxing gloves. The only fun of that was that Otto actually was rather fond of his boxing gloves, and that they were red to match the Dannebrog.

Otto, on the other hand, spent a whole eight days thinking before making up his mind.

Had it not been Otto, and had his scheme not been so sublime, we would all have become mad at him. For while he was doing his thinking, we again became aware of Pierre Anthon's hollering up there in the plum tree.

"You go to school to get a job, and you get a job to take time off to do nothing. Why not do nothing to begin with?" he shouted, and spat a plum stone at us.

It was like the heap of meaning began shrinking and losing some of the meaning, and the thought was unbearable.

"Just you wait and see!" I yelled as loud as I could, dodging at once a squashy plum that came flying.

"There's nothing to wait for," Pierre Anthon hollered back condescendingly. "And there's nothing at all worth seeing. And the longer you wait, the less there'll be!"

I covered my ears and hurried the rest of the way to school.

But there was no comfort to be found at school that day; the teachers were cross with us. They had a pretty good idea it was our class that was behind the disappearance of the snake in formaldehyde. How could Henrik have been so dumb as to snatch it right after one of our biology lessons?

We all had to stay behind an hour every day after school until we revealed what we'd done with it. Everyone, that is, except Henrik, for Henrik's father was sure it couldn't have been Henrik.

Butter-up! Butter-up! Little Henrik Butter-up!

How we cursed him and looked forward to the day the heap was finished, and Pierre Anthon had seen it, and we could tell it like it was, so little Henrik Butter-up could get what was coming to him.

In the meantime he just went strutting around the place.

Strutting, trotting, rutting!

At least until Huge Hans got his hands on him and slapped his ears and cheeks so that he had to beg for mercy, and was granted it because his father in the meantime had retracted and repealed our detention.

"Elise's baby brother," Otto finally announced, and it was like a gust of wind passed through the saw-mill.

It was afternoon. We were sitting at the foot of the heap of meaning, and we all knew what it entailed, what Otto was saying. Elise's baby brother had died when he was only two years old. And Elise's baby brother was buried in the churchyard up on the hill. What Otto was saying meant that we had to dig up the coffin containing Elise's baby brother and lug it down the hill all the way out to the sawmill and the heap of meaning. And it had to be done under cover of darkness if we were to pull it off without being found out.

We looked at Elise.

Maybe we were hoping she would say something
that made the venture impossible.

Elise said nothing. Her baby brother had been sick from the time he was born to the time he died, and in all that time Elise's parents had done nothing but care for him, while Elise had hung out on the streets and achieved poor exam grades and become bad company before eventually going to live with her grandparents. Until, that is, her baby brother died six months ago, and Elise moved home to her parents again.

I don't think Elise was too sad about her baby brother being dead. And I don't think she was too sad that he was going onto the heap of meaning. I think Elise was more afraid of her parents than of us, and that that was why after a long silence she said:

"We can't."

"Of course we can," Otto replied.

"No, we mustn't." Elise wrinkled her brow.

"Must has nothing to do with it. We're doing it, and that's that."

"But it's sacrilege," protested Holy Karl, and it was he more than Elise who was objecting. "We'll be invoking the wrath of God," he explained. "The dead are to rest in peace."

Peace. More peace. Rest in peace.

Holy Karl's objections were in vain.

"It's going to take six of us," Otto declared, undaunted. "Four taking turns to dig and two to keep lookout."

We looked at one another. There were no volunteers.

"We'll draw lots," Otto said.

There was a long discussion about how to make the draw. Eventually we agreed on drawing cards; the four who drew the highest cards were going to the churchyard. Four, because Otto and Elise obviously had to be among the six.

I offered to run home and get a deck of cards, but time was getting on, so we decided to put it off until the next day. On the birght side, the excavation itself would be done and over with by the following evening. Barring rain.

I've always liked a game of cards and have always had lots of different decks. As soon as dinner was over I went into my room, closed the door, and took out all my playing cards.

There were the classical ones in blue and red, but it wasn't going to be them. Then there were the miniature decks, which didn't seem right either. And it couldn't be the ones with the horses' heads on the back, or the ones with the clowns, or the ones where the jacks and kings looked like Arab sultans. Eventually there was only one deck left. But this one seemed fitting, for the reverse side was black and edged with a thin gilt line, and since they had almost never been used, the gilt edging was fully intact and still shiny. These were the ones.

I put away the remaining decks and spread out the gilt-edged playing cards on my desk. I examined each carefully. There was something ominous about them, not just the face cards, with the witch-like queen and the king with his piercing eyes, and not just the way-too-black spades and the claw-like clubs, but also the blue-red diamonds and hearts that most of all made me think about exactly what it was I didn't want to think about.

Or maybe I was just starting to get a little rickety

at the thought of digging up little Emil's coffin.

Up. Down. And bucketsful of something I didn't want to think about.

There were two options.

Either I could remove a deuce and hide it away in my pocket and then somehow swap the card I drew tomorrow with the deuce. Or I could mark one of the deuces in such a way that I'd be able to pick it out when it was my turn to draw, and in a way no-one else would notice.

Even though I didn't know how I was going to mark the card without it being noticeable, I chose the second option. If anyone decided to count the cards before drawing lots, I'd be found out there and then. The safest thing was to mark them.

After long deliberations, I scraped away the gilt edge of all four corners of the two of spades. To be on the safe side, I then did the same on the three remaining deuces. It looked like random wear and tear. I was on the safe side now. It wouldn't be me digging up Elise's baby brother in the middle of the night.

———

The next day there was an odd kind of suppressed restlessness about the class.

There were no jokes being told, no-one sending notes around, no-one throwing paper planes. Not even when we had a substitute for Maths. Yet there was still a whole lot of noise. Chairs rocking backwards and forwards, tables being shoved first one way then another, pens scratching at table edges, and pencils getting chewed at the ends.

The lessons dragged on and went by too fast all at once.

It was the afternoon we were nervous about. Everyone except me. I smiled calmly from behind my desk and gained a couple of merits for being the only one able to pull myself together to answer Eskildsen's questions about weather, winds and water in America, both North and South. Once in a while I let my finger run along the black, gilt-edged cards in my bag just to be sure I could still make out the rough edges of four of them.

When the bell rang for the end of the final lesson

we had already packed our bags, and we set out in threes in different directions. There were four different routes we could take to the sawmill, and we never went there in groups of more than a few at a time. We didn't want any grown-ups getting suspicious and starting to nose around.

It took only twenty minutes from the bell ringing until the last three arrived. I pulled out the black cards from my schoolbag and handed them to Jon-Johan. He studied them for a long while and I had to look away so as not to stare too obviously at his hands as they seemingly felt for telltale marks. Yet I couldn't help but smile as he eventually signalled his satisfaction and started to carefully shuffle the deck.

Jon-Johan cut and placed the stack on a board laid across two sawhorses.

"Right," he said. "To avoid cheating we all take the topmost card. Aces high, deuces low. Everybody in line..."

Jon-Johan added something, but what it was I didn't hear. Suddenly I had to pee badly, I was freezing and felt like I was about to be sick. If only

I'd taken the other option and now had a deuce in my back pocket!

There was nothing that could be done. I had to step into line somewhere in the middle behind Ur-sula-Marie and could only play along.

Everyone was fidgety with nerves, and it was as if the line was moving even when it was standing still. Only Otto and Elise looked unmoved as they stood there alongside us, watching and sniggering and making fun, unperturbed by the fact that no-one was inclined to join in.

Gerda drew the first card and looked neither relieved nor disappointed, just held it against her chest as soon as she'd noted what she had drawn. Huge Hans burst out laughing and held up a three so we all could see. Sebastian laughed too, but not quite as loud; he'd drawn the eight of diamonds. One by one, the line moved forward, some were ecstatic, others turned silent, but most did the same as Gerda and held their cards close to their chests while the others drew.

Then it was Ursula-Marie's turn. She hesitated for a moment before lifting the uppermost card and heaving a sigh of relief. She had drawn a five. It was my turn.

I knew straightaway it wasn't a deuce on top. The first visible rough edge lay several cards down. For a moment I thought about toppling the stack like it was an accident, then gathering up the cards with the deuce just happening to be on top. But Richard was rushing me from behind, and all I could do was pick up the topmost card with its unblemished gilt edging shining at every corner.

Ace of spades.

Thirteen out of thirteen is thirteen.

I didn't faint.

But the rest of the draw took place without me registering a thing. I didn't come round until I found myself standing in a circle together with Otto, Elise, Jon-Johan, Richard, and Holy Karl. From now on, Otto was in charge.

"We meet up at eleven by Richard's bike shed. From there it's only a short way to the churchyard."

"This is not a good idea," Holy Karl stuttered.

"And I can get expelled from the Mission."

"I don't think it's a good idea either." Elise, too, was getting cold feet. "Isn't there something else I can give up? My watch, for example." Elise stretched out her arm so everyone could see the red wristwatch her father had bought her the time she moved in with her grandparents.

Otto shook his head.

"My Discman, then?" Elise patted her jacket pocket, where we knew she kept the little marvel that no-one else in class could match.

I don't think Elise was very sad about having to dig up her baby brother. I think Elise was afraid her parents would find out and send her away for good. For when Otto refused to yield, she didn't insist, but merely said:

"We have to remember exactly how the flowers were so we can put them back again afterward."

Otto now ordered Jon-Johan to bring a spade along; the other one we could borrow from Richard's parents' shed. Holy Karl was to bring his trailer, and Elise and I were to make sure we had flashlights with us. Otto himself would take a broom to brush away the dirt from the coffin.

Holy Karl looked badly affected by the mention of the coffin, and I think he might even have cried had Otto not at that very moment concluded that it was all agreed: eleven o'clock at Richard's bike shed.

X

I'd set my alarm to go off at ten-thirty, but I needn't have bothered. I never managed to fall asleep, just lay in bed with my eyes open for more than an hour and a half before it was time to get up. At exactly twenty-five past ten I climbed out of bed, turned off the alarm and put on my jeans and a sweater. I stuck my feet into my rubber boots and grabbed the flashlight I'd put out ready on the desk. I could hear the faint sound of the television from inside the living-room. Fortunately, ours was a single-storey home. I was able to crawl out of the window in my room without being noticed. I jammed a book into place to stop the window from closing again, and then I was away.

It was colder than I'd reckoned.

I was freezing in my thin sweater and had to beat my arms to get warm. I'd considered staying in bed, but it wouldn't have helped. Otto had sworn that if anyone failed to turn up at Richard's, the others would simply return home and leave whoever it was to do the job alone the following evening. Just the thought of being alone in the churchyard after dark was enough to make me hurry. Running helped against the cold, too.

It was only ten to eleven when I got to Richard's bike shed. Jon-Johan and Holy Karl were already there. Before long, Elise turned up too, and only shortly afterwards Richard appeared in the mudroom doorway of his house. Otto arrived on the stroke of eleven.

"Let's go," he said as soon as he'd made sure everything was ready: two spades, flashlights, and Holy Karl's trailer.

None of us spoke as we crept our way through the streets to the church.

The town was silent too.

There was never much going on in the evenings

in Tæring, and nothing at all late on a regular Tuesday. We stuck close to the garden hedges as we walked along Richard's street, turned down the road where Sebastian and Laura lived, ran past the bakery and ducked down the path behind Ursula-Marie's house on Tæring Hovedgade, and arrived at the churchyard hill having encountered nothing but two amorous cats that Otto chased off with a kick.

The churchyard hill was steep, and the path between the graves was covered with gravel. We had to leave the trailer at the iron gates. Holy Karl didn't like it much, but Otto promised to beat him up if he started acting up.

The streets had been dimly and rather sinisterly illuminated by the yellow streetlamps. Tall fir trees sheltered the churchyard from the street, and although they may well have protected us from any inquisitive gaze, they also screened off the street lighting, which we suddenly found ourselves in want of. There was no more light than came from the new moon and the small hexagonal lamp at the entrance to the church. And of course the two beams our flashlights cut in the dark.

Dark. Darker. Afraid of the dark.

I didn't like being in the churchyard to begin with. At this time of night it was quite beyond endurance. The gravel crunched sharply beneath our feet however carefully we tiptoed. I kept counting to a hundred over and over inside my head, first forward, then backward, then forward again, and so on, and so on, and then once more again.

Fifty-two, fifty-three, fifty-four...

We had to search around in the dark before Elise got her bearings and was able to lead us to her baby brother's grave. Seventy-seven, seventy-eight, seventy-nine...And there it was: EMIL JENSEN, DEARLY BELOVED SON AND BROTHER, JANUARY 3, 1990 – FEBRUARY 21, 1992, read the inscription on the headstone.

I glanced at Elise and would have wagered she didn't go in for the part about the dearly beloved brother. Nonetheless, I could easily see why he had to go on the heap. A baby brother was something special no matter what. Even if he may not have been all that loved.

The stone was marble and very white and beautiful with two doves on top and red, yellow, and violet flowers placed in front. I almost began to cry and had to look up at the sky and the stars and the new moon and think about what Pierre Anthon had said that same morning: that the moon took twenty-eight days to circle the Earth, whereas the Earth took a year to circle the sun.

That made the tears go away, but I didn't dare look at the stone and the doves again. Now Otto sent Elise and me off in separate directions to keep a lookout. He kept the flashlights. The boys would need them to see where they were digging, he said, and we had to find our way between the graves to the end of the church with only the light of the moon, which made everything seem ghostlike and almost blue. Elise stood guard at the rear entrance on the other side of the church, not far from the rectory, but very far from my own position. Talking to each other was obviously out of the question. We didn't even have the comfort of being able to see each other.

I tried to concentrate on studying the church. The stone walls were rough and white, there were carvings in the light-colored timber doors, and way up high were stained-glass windows which at this time of night simply appeared dark. I started counting again. One, two, three...

An odd, hollow sound came from the grave behind me every time one of the spades struck the earth. A thud, and then a whishing sound as the soil slid from the spade. *Thud, whish, thud, whish.* To begin with, the two spades worked quickly in succession. Then came a sharp clash. The boys had hit the coffin, and now work progressed more slowly. I knew they were edging close around the casket in order to dig as little as possible. The thought sent shivers down my spine. I shuddered and tried not to think about it again. Instead, I looked across at the fir trees and set out to count them.

There were eighteen tall ones and seven smaller ones lining the path from the street up to the church. Their branches waved slightly in a breeze I couldn't feel. But then again I was standing sheltered behind the wall of the churchyard. I took two

JANNE TELLER

small steps forward, one to the side and two back. And again, this time to the other side. And once more in a little dance made up inside my head. One, two, step to the side. One, two, back. One, two, step to the side...

I halted abruptly.

I'd heard something. Like gravel being pressed gently underfoot. I stared down the path but could see nothing. If only I'd had the flashlight. There it was again.

Cruuuunch.

It was coming from the bottom of the path, down by the gate. I felt an irresistible urge to pee and was just about to run back over to the boys. But then I remembered what Otto had said and knew he'd cuff me one if I came running all of a sudden. I took a deep breath, cupped my hands together and made a deep, hooting sound by blowing air through the crack between my thumbs into the hollow of my palms.

"*Uuuuuh,*" came the faint sound.

The gravel crunched again and I hooted as hard as I could.

79

"*Uuuuuh. Uuuuuh.*"

Otto appeared beside me.

"What's wrong?" he whispered.

I was so scared I was unable to answer, I just lifted my arm and pointed down the path.

"Come on," Otto commanded, and since I was just as scared of not obeying Otto as I was of whatever it was that was making the noise, I followed him off behind the fir trees where the light was dimmest.

We snuck a few steps, then Otto stopped and looked around. I stood behind him and couldn't see a thing. There was nothing there, and Otto continued on. We moved slowly so as not to make the slightest sound. My heart was pounding, thumping in my ears, and it felt like we were stealing around there between the trunks of the fir trees for ages.

Then Otto pushed aside the branches and stepped out onto the path.

"Ha," he scoffed. I peered over his shoulder and felt stupid.

It was Cinderella. Sørensen's old dog. After the old man had died, Cinderella had refused to reside anywhere else than on top of her master's grave. The dog had grown inquisitive at the sound of the spades and had shuffled slowly and sedately off up the hill on her arthritic old legs. Fortunately, she wasn't one for barking. She just stared at us some, and sniffed at my legs. I patted her on the head and returned to my post.

Not long after, it was Otto who signalled.

They were finished digging. The little coffin had been put out onto the gravel path and looked abandoned and so awfully sad, but there was no time to think about that, there was another problem. The boys had shovelled all the earth they'd dug up back into the grave, but the hole was still only three quarters full.

A law of physics we had never learned: when a physical body is removed from the ground, the level of earth at the place occupied by the body will diminish relative to the body's volume.

Anybody going anywhere near little Emil Jensen's grave couldn't help but notice that little Emil

Jensen was no longer occupying it. Now Elise began to cry and wouldn't stop, no matter how much Otto insisted.

We stood a while without knowing what to do. Then I figured we could roll a couple of headstones from the other graves into the hole and cover them up with earth. The church warden was going to wonder about the missing stones, but he was never going to guess they were at the bottom of Emil Jensen's grave. All we had to do was make sure we put all the flowers back as they were before.

It took us a good while and a whole lot of toil to get the stones loose and roll them over to little Emil's grave. We left the ones closest by in case anyone noticed the earth had just been dug. But down they went eventually, with a good heap of earth on top, and gravel topmost of all, and then the flowers, which had suffered some underway, but which would just pass after we'd brushed them down a bit with Otto's broom.

The town hall clock struck midnight exactly as we finished up and turned towards the coffin.

I stiffened, and even in the dark I could see

the boys grow pale. The town hall clock had a deep, hollow resonance, and each stroke echoed through the graveyard like some ponderous, ghostly appeal.

Come! Come! Come!

None of us moved.

I could neither look nor close my eyes and just stared stiffly at Jon-Johan like he was the only image I dared admit to my retina. I didn't count the strokes, but it felt like there were many more than twelve. After an age the last one died away and silence prevailed once more.

We looked at each other nervously. Then Jon-Johan cleared his throat and pointed at the coffin.

"Let's get out of here," he said. I noted his subtle avoidance of the word coffin.

The coffin must have been very fine and white when Elise's baby brother had been put into it. Now the white finish was blistered and cracked and no longer fine at all. There was a worm crawling in some earth at one of the corners, and Holy Karl refused to carry until Otto had brushed it away. Then they bore the coffin, the four of them:

Otto and Holy Karl on one side, Richard and Jon-Johan on the other. Elise, who had stopped crying when the town hall clock had struck, walked ahead and lit the way with her flashlight, while I brought up the rear with mine.

The coffin was heavier than they'd imagined, and the boys were panting and sweating, but Otto wouldn't let them rest until we were all the way down to the street. It was no loss to me. I could see no reason to hang about in the churchyard more than was absolutely necessary.

Behind me there was a crunching of gravel.

Sørensen's Cinderella plodded slowly along after us as if she were the mourner in the procession. To begin with it was comforting and kind of made us feel braver, but when we got down to the street and the coffin had been handled into place on the trailer, we were somewhat unnerved to see her still following on behind.

———

It wouldn't do for the church warden to discover the next morning that not only was he missing two gravestones, but Cinderella was gone too. There was nothing we could do about it, though. No sooner had one of us taken her back to the churchyard than she turned around and followed us again. After we had tried to shake her off four times, we gave up and decided she could come along until she turned back herself. Which she didn't. When we arrived at the sawmill, turned the code on the padlock, and opened up, Cinderella slipped in ahead of us.

I turned on the lights and the boys stepped in with the coffin between them. In the bright neon light it didn't seem so scary anymore. It's just a dead child with some wood around it, I thought to myself as I considered more closely the coffin, which had now been placed at the foot of the heap of meaning, it being too heavy to be put on top.

We were too tired to worry any more about Cinderella, so we just let her be, turned off the lights, locked up and scuttled away back through the town. Reaching the end of my street, I said goodnight to the others and hurried off, rather more at ease than I had been setting out.

The book was still jammed in the window, and I climbed inside and into bed without waking anyone in the house.

XI

How they stared when they saw the coffin with Sørensen's Cinderella on top.

The six of us who had been at the churchyard may well have felt like falling asleep at school that day, but we certainly weren't hanging our heads. On the contrary! The story was passed around the class and around again in an ever-increasing whisper until Eskildsen became furious and yelled at us to be quiet. Everything went still for a moment, and then it all started off again and Eskildsen had to holler at us some more.

It felt like an eternity before the final lesson was

over and we could set off in our different directions to the sawmill. But then there was no end to the heroics and the events of the previous night, the churchyard plunging deeper into darkness, looming larger and more forbidding as the story was told and told again.

In the days that followed, there was no-one anywhere in the town who wasn't talking about the vandalism at the churchyard.

Two gravestones had been stolen, someone had trampled around on little Emil Jensen's grave, and Sørensen's Cinderella had disappeared. The latter event was a source of very little regret; after all, it was a disgrace having that old mongrel going about the churchyard urinating on the gravestones and depositing stuff that was worse who knows where.

No-one suspected us.

My mum did ask me about the gravel and the dirt on the carpet in my room. But I just said I'd been playing with Sofie on the field behind her house and had forgotten to take off my boots when

I came home. And even if I did get bawled out for the boots, it was nothing compared to what would have happened if my mom had found out where I'd really been.

It was Cinderella who gave us the most trouble.

She refused to leave little Emil's coffin for more than just a few minutes at a time. She must have thought Sørensen's remains were inside. Whatever, we were unable to let her out of the sawmill during the daytime. If anyone saw her together with one of us, they'd be sure to get suspicious about matters at the churchyard. Sofie, who lived closest to the sawmill, couldn't get away to walk Cinderella after dark. She wasn't allowed out late, and her parents were already of the opinion that she was spending far too much time at the old sawmill. It was Elise who solved the problem.

It was like Elise had grown fonder of her dead baby brother after his coffin had been placed under our care. And perhaps it was Cinderella keeping guard by the coffin that made Elise especially fond of her. No matter the reason, Elise offered to go out to the sawmill every evening and take the dog out for air. It was mid-September now, and dark by eight-thirty, so there was just enough time for her to be back home before bedtime. Her parents didn't care much one way or the other if she stayed out late, Elise explained, and looked as if she didn't know if that was good or bad.

"There's one other thing," she added.

We stared at her, mouths wide open. With all our nerves about the matter at the churchyard, we'd forgotten that it was now Elise's turn to choose the next thing to be going on the heap of meaning.

"Ursula-Marie's hair!"

I looked at Ursula-Marie, who had immediately brought her hand up to her thick blue braids and now opened her mouth in a protest she knew was futile.

"I've got some scissors!" Hussain announced, laughing. He held up his Swiss Army knife and pulled out the scissors.

"I'll do the cutting," said Elise.

"They're my scissors, I'll do it," Hussain insisted, and they agreed on doing half each.

Blue. Bluer. Bluest.

Ursula-Marie sat quite still and didn't say a word as they cut, but the tears rolled down her cheeks, and it was like the blue of her hair reflected in her lips, which she gnawed until they bled.

I looked the other way so as not to cry too.

Cutting off Ursula-Marie's hair was worse than cutting off Samson's. Without her hair, Ursula-Marie would no longer be Ursula-Marie with her six blue braids, which meant that she no longer would be Ursula-Marie at all. I wondered whether that was the reason the six blue braids were part of the meaning, but I didn't care to say it out loud. Or leave it unspoken. Ursula-Marie was my friend, even if she no longer was Ursula-Marie with her six blue braids, peerless and all her own.

First Elise cut off one braid. Then Hussain cut off another. It was hard work, the scissors were blunt and Ursula-Marie's hair was thick. It took them twenty minutes to get through all six. By that time, Ursula-Marie looked like someone who had become lost on her way to the asylum.

The severed braids were placed in a pile on top of the heap of meaning.

Blue. Bluer. Bluest.

———

Ursula-Marie sat for a long time looking at her braids.

There were no longer tears on her cheeks. Instead, her eyes were glowing with rage. She turned calmly to Hussain and in a gentle voice, her teeth only moderately clenched, said:

"Your prayer mat!"

XII

Hussain kicked up a storm.

Hussain kicked up a storm to the extent that we finally had to beat him up. "We" being Otto and Huge Hans. The rest of us watched. It took a while, but eventually Hussain just lay there with his face in the sawdust and Otto on his back. He wasn't saying anything any more. When they let him get to his feet he looked terrified, almost like he was shaking. But somehow it wasn't Otto or Huge Hans he was scared of.

Who it was, we didn't discover until Hussain had handed over his prayer mat in tears and then hadn't come to school for a whole week. When finally he showed up again, he was black and blue and yellow and green all over, and his left arm was broken. He was not a good Muslim, his father had told him, and then had beaten the life out of him.

That wasn't the worst.

The worst was that he wasn't a good Muslim.

A bad Muslim! No Muslim! No-one!

Something in Hussain seemed to have been destroyed.

He went round dragging his feet with his head bowed, and whereas before he'd always dished out his fair share of knocks and shoves, now he wouldn't even defend himself if someone went for him.

I have to say it was a beautiful mat. The patterns were interwoven, red and blue and grey, and it was so fine and soft to the touch that Cinderella looked like she was going to abandon little Emil's coffin. But then Jon-Johan laid the mat at the top of the heap of meaning, where Cinderella couldn't reach it. That helped. Cinderella stayed put.

At first Hussain wasn't saying what the next in line had to give up. He just shook his head despondently when we began to pressure him.

Pierre Anthon's hollering was getting to us, and Hussain would have to get a move on. It was already October, and we were far from being done. We wanted it over with, and there were still five of us to go.

Eventually, when Hussain was unable to put it off any longer, he pointed to Huge Hans and said quietly:

"The yellow bike."

Hardly a big deal, even if the bicycle was brand-new and neon yellow and a racer, and Huge Hans was beside himself and waited two whole days before he came and leaned it up against the heap of meaning in the old sawmill. Still, a little was better than nothing, and at least now we were able to go on to the rest.

Had we known that giving up his bike would make Huge Hans so furious that he would do something terrible, then some of us may well have told Hussain to think of something else. But we didn't know, and we insisted on Huge Hans handing over his neon yellow bike, just like Hussain had said.

Sofie was one of those who pressured the most.

She shouldn't have done that.

XIII

I can hardly bring myself to tell what it was Sofie had to give up. It was something only a boy could think of, and it was so gross and repugnant that the rest of us almost all pleaded on her behalf. Sofie herself said hardly anything, just no and no and no, and shook her head again and again, and the rest of her was shaking some too.

Huge Hans was merciless.

And of course we had to admit that we had all been quite unyielding when he had been forced to hand over his neon yellow bike.

It wasn't the same, we said.

"How do you know my neon yellow bike doesn't mean as much to me as Sofie's innocence means to her?"

We didn't.

So even though we had our doubts, it was eventually agreed that Huge Hans was going to help her lose it the following evening at the old sawmill. Four of the boys were to stay behind to lend a hand if necessary. The rest of us would be sent home to make sure we couldn't come to her rescue.

———

It was a dreadful day at school.

Sofie sat white as the classroom walls at her desk and said nothing, not even when some of the girls tried to comfort her. No-one else dared say anything either for thinking about what was going to happen to Sofie, and it was almost worse than when we were making trouble, for Eskildsen had never known us so quiet all at once in the same lesson. He was beginning to suspect, and started going on about our class behaving very oddly ever since the beginning of the school year. He was right, but fortunately he didn't connect it with Pierre Anthon's empty desk. If he'd started on about Pierre Anthon, I'm not sure we could have kept things up.

While Eskildsen went on and on about our strange behaviour since August, I turned my head to look at Sofie. I don't think I would have blamed her if she'd told on us at that point. But she didn't. She sat completely still, all pale in the face like little Emil's coffin must have been when it was new, and yet calm and almost collected like I imagined a saint would look who was about to meet her death.

I started thinking about how it had all begun,

and how Pierre Anthon was still yelling at us from up there in his plum tree, mornings and afternoons and whenever we passed by Tæringvej 25. It wasn't just us who were going crazy from all this. It sounded like he himself would be losing it if we didn't get him out of that tree soon.

"Chimpanzees have almost exactly the same brain and DNA as us," he'd hollered the day before, and started swinging around in the branches of the plum tree. "There's nothing the least special about being human." And this morning he'd said: "There are six billion people on Earth. Way too many! But in the year 2025 there'll be eight and a half billion. The best thing we can do for the future of the world is to die!"

He must have gained all that knowledge from the newspapers. I don't see the point, collecting all that knowledge others have already discovered. It's enough to make anybody lose heart who has not yet grown up and found out anything for themselves. But grown-ups love collecting knowledge, the more the better, and it doesn't even matter if it's other people's knowledge and something you only learn from reading. Sofie was doing right to grin and bear it. There was definitely something that mattered in spite of everything, even if that something was something you had to lose.

I don't know exactly what happened the night Huge Hans helped Sofie give up the innocence. The next day there was just a smidgeon of blood and some slime on a chequered handkerchief lying at the top of the heap of meaning, and Sofie was walking a bit funny like it hurt when she moved her legs. Nonetheless, it was Sofie who looked proud and inapproachable, while Huge Hans was running around trying to please her.

"He probably wants to do it again," Gerda whispered in my ear and giggled, completely forgetting that she wasn't talking to me because of the matter of Oscarlittle.

I didn't reply, but tried later on to get Sofie to tell what had happened and how it had been.

She wouldn't tell me anything. Just walked around looking like she'd found out a secret that may have been terrible but which nonetheless had handed her the key to something of great meaning.

Great meaning? Greater meaning? Greatest meaning?

There were only three to go before we could show the heap of meaning to Pierre Anthon if he promised never again to sit in his plum tree and holler at us: Holy Karl, Pretty Rosa and Jon-Johan.

Sofie chose Holy Karl. He was to deliver Jesus on the Cross.

XIV

Jesus on the Cross wasn't just Holy Karl's God almighty, he was also the most sacred thing in Tæring Church, and Tæring Church was itself the most sacred thing there was in Tæring. And so Jesus on the Cross was the most sacred thing any of us could imagine – if any of us believed in all that. Perhaps he was anyway, regardless of what we believed.

Jesus on the Cross was a statue that hung on the wall just behind the altar and made the small kids scared and the old folks teary-eyed with its bowed head and its crown of thorns and the drops of blood that ran together in majestic streams down the sacred face that was twisted in pain and divinity, and the nails that fixed the hands and feet to the cross, which was made of rosewood and so very, very fine, according to what the priest said. Even I, who insisted that Jesus and Our Lord did not exist and therefore meant nothing, knew that Jesus on the Rosewood Cross meant a great deal. Especially to Holy Karl.

He was going to need help.

Help is thine. Help is ours. Help is us.

Once again I took my playing cards with me to the sawmill, this time the deck with the clowns on the reverse. And once again we drew lots.

This time it was Ursula-Marie, Jon-Johan, Richard and Maiken who drew the highest cards and who therefore were going to help Holy Karl, regardless of Holy Karl maintaining that this was something we couldn't and mustn't do. He softened up some when Jon-Johan said that Karl had the code to the padlock and could come by and pray to his Jesus on the Cross anytime at the sawmill. And that we would of course be returning Jesus to the church as soon as we were done with him.

I wasn't a part of it, but what Ursula-Marie without her six blue braids told me in a hushed voice on the Monday morning in the music lesson while the others were listening to Beethoven and nearly drowning her out was that it hadn't all worked out according to plan.

Holy Karl had hidden himself away in the church as agreed following the late Sunday service. And when the church had grown still and was locked up and everyone had gone, Ursula-Marie, Jon-Johan, Richard and Maiken had come and given three short and three long knocks at the door and Holy Karl had let them in. But then it all started going wrong.

First Holy Karl had started to cry.

It was when the others had crawled over the prie-dieu and gone behind the altar, and he sobbed and begged so much that they had to let him stay behind on the other side. And Maiken had to stay with him to make sure he didn't run off. And it didn't help no matter how many times she told him she'd never yet seen Jesus or Our Lord in her telescope, even though she'd looked all over, and neither had any of the great astrophysicists in this entire world. Holy Karl just covered his ears and howled so loud he couldn't hear what she was saying, and Maiken eventually just had to give up. She was scared, too, that Holy Karl's howling would get heard by someone outside the church.

Jon-Johan and Richard had meanwhile been trying to loosen Jesus on the Rosewood Cross.

But Jesus was well-fastened, and however much they sweated over him he wasn't moving. Then Ursula-Marie had gone over to Jesus. And as she placed her hand on the foot of Jesus with the nail and the blood it was like she burnt herself. Ursula-Marie had to admit that even if she didn't believe in all that hokum, she certainly got a real scare. The church was so strangely empty and infinite inside, and at once it was like the Jesus figure was coming alive. Ever so slowly without anyone even touching him, Jesus slid on his own with a scraping sound all the way down the wall and hit the floor with a bump and broke that same leg that Ursula-Marie had just touched.

That was about the eeriest thing Ursula-Marie

had ever seen in her life.

They all felt like taking to their heels, but now they'd come this far they couldn't just let Jesus lie there on the floor. So despite his astonishing weight they managed to lift him free and haul him over to the prie-dieu and tip him over onto the other side. It was almost unnatural how heavy Jesus was, and however much Holy Karl was against it, he had to help carry. So now they were five to carry, and still they were barely able to haul Jesus out into the street and the waiting trailer.

By then it was seven thirty and dark as they went through the streets with Jesus on the Rose-wood Cross in Holy Karl's trailer. Even so, they had to stop a couple of times to hide behind trees and hedges so as not to be seen by passers-by.

Holy Karl howled all the way through Tæring and out to the old sawmill and kept on repeat-ing that they couldn't do this. And Ursula-Marie, whose hand was still stinging from the burn, was beginning to agree. And Maiken kept on and on re-peating that she'd never seen either Jesus nor Our Lord in her telescope, almost like what she was mostly doing was trying to remind herself. And even Jon-Johan, who normally wouldn't shy at anything, was nervous and abrupt and couldn't get to the sawmill quick enough. Only Richard seemed unperturbed, though only until they reached the sawmill and the code on the lock didn't work. Then he went berserk, yelling and screeching and kicking at the door to the sawmill and then at the trailer, so Jesus on the Rosewood Cross fell and broke his other leg too.

Holy Karl went completely hysterical and said that it was blasphemy to break the legs of Jesus, and now they couldn't give Jesus on the Rosewood Cross back to the church after they'd convinced Pierre Anthon that Jesus was part of the meaning, and that Holy Karl would never be able to show his face in church ever again. Then Jon-Johan had barked at Holy Karl and told him to shut his mouth, for wasn't it Jesus himself who said that all sinners would be forgiven if only they believed in him? And this actually made Holy Karl shut up and almost smile again, and then they got the lock to work since they'd just remembered the code wrong.

But now a new problem arose.

When they lugged Jesus on the Rosewood Cross into the sawmill, Sørensen's Cinderella went amok.

Amok. More amok. Amokker-fokker, stupid dog!

Cinderella started barking like crazy and snapping at them every time they tried to carry Jesus over to the heap of meaning. And eventually they had to go home and leave Jesus lying in the mouldy sawdust in the middle of the floor.

It was a real problem, the matter of Jesus and the rosewood cross in the sawdust.

There were others besides Holy Karl who didn't think it proper. Cinderella, however, didn't care whether it was proper or not and refused to let Jesus anywhere near the heap of meaning. It didn't matter what we did.

Did. Diddle. Diddly-dog!

No amount of coaxing or tidbits made any impression on her, and none of us wanted to get on the wrong side of those snapping jaws. After several hours we were feeling like giving up and going home. It was getting close to supper time. But then I remembered the night we'd taken the coffin with little Emil Jensen inside.

"Maybe she thinks it's Jesus who took Sørensen away from her," I suggested.

"So it was, too" Otto said, laughing.

"No, seriously," I persisted.

"Yeah, seriously," Otto laughed, and then I got mad.

Elise broke in and said I was right, and that we'd never get Jesus and the rosewood cross onto the heap of meaning as long as Cinderella was keeping guard of it.

We thought about what she said for a long while, for Jesus on the Cross somehow wasn't going to matter much in the final count if he didn't get onto the heap.

"We'll just chop him up into smaller pieces," Huge Hans suggested.

"No!" exclaimed Holy Karl.

And even though none of us could care less about

Holy Karl as far as this was concerned, neither did any of us think it was a good idea. It was like the meaning would go out of Jesus if we chopped him up into pieces.

"Then we'll paint him black, so Cinderella won't recognise him," Sebastian suggested.

"No, it won't be the same," Jon-Johan protested, and all of us agreed with him: a black Jesus wasn't quite the same.

"What if we put Jesus on the heap while I'm out walking Cinderella?" suggested Elise, and now no-one had any objections.

The same evening after supper we went back to the sawmill.

Elise put Cinderella on the leash and as soon as they were out of the door, Jon-Johan and Huge Hans took a hold of Jesus and lugged him over to the heap of meaning. Jesus was too heavy to be put on top, so instead they placed him so he stood leaned up against the heap. The Dannebrog was aloft, a boxing glove slid down and disappeared from sight, the snake in formaldehyde rolled ominously, and Oscarlittle squealed.

Jesus on the Rosewood Cross was a part of the heap of meaning!

Out of consideration for Cinderella's feelings we'd placed Jesus as far from little Emil's coffin as he could get, way over on the opposite side of the heap. Not that I think it made any difference where Jesus was put for what Cinderella did next.

Elise gave her three short and three long knocks at the door of the sawmill.

We all moved well away from the heap of meaning. Jon-Johan opened the door and Elise walked in with Cinderella plodding slowly along behind her. The dog was puffing and panting like a boiled-out kettle and looked like she was going to collapse any minute. But no sooner was the leash removed than she lifted her head, nosed the air like a sprite-ly young pup and trotted elegantly and without effort, her tail aloft, over to the heap of meaning, where she sniffed a moment at Jesus on the Rosewood Cross, before squatting halfway up the cross and peeing on Jesus right about the midriff.

Pee-pee. Piddly-piss. Oh, my Lord!

Gerda giggled. The rest of us uttered not a sound.

The consequences of Cinderella's behaviour were quite incalculable. We would never be able to return a pissed-on Jesus statue to the church.

Nevertheless, one by one we all began to laugh. All that piety was just too comical with Cinderella's yellow fluid running down the sides and onto the broken stumps that had been legs, then dripping on down into the sawdust. And anyway, with two broken legs, Jesus wasn't doing too good to begin with.

We laughed and laughed, and there was a good feeling now, and after a while Sofie went and got her stereo tape-deck so we could have some music. And we sang and screeched and had a real time of ourselves until we realized it was past nine o'clock.

The tape was turned off and we flew off home in all directions. Imagine if some of the grown-ups had gone out looking for us and heard the noise from the old sawmill.

XV

We weren't expecting much of Holy Karl, but this time he surprised us: he wanted Cinderella's head.

Weird.

Especially because Cinderella didn't belong to anyone.

To be sure, the dog meant most to Elise, but Elise had already given up her baby brother's coffin. Otherwise, only Pretty Rosa and Jon-Johan were left, and why should giving up Cinderella's head mean more to either of them than to the rest of us?

Holy Karl insisted.

"Oh, come on, Karl," said Otto.

"Cinderella's head," Holy Karl demanded.

"Get serious, Karl!" said Elise.

"Cinderella's head," Holy Karl demanded.

"Quit fooling around, Karl," said Maiken.

"Cinderella's head!" Holy Karl demanded, and continued demanding regardless of what the rest of us were saying.

Truth be told, we knew why.

Ever since Jesus had been dragged onto the heap of meaning, five days ago now, Cinderella had been using the rosewood cross as her personal toilet, both for one thing and another. Jesus on the Rosewood Cross had already lost a good deal of his sacredness with the broken legs and all, and now with the dogged efforts of Cinderella there surely wasn't much hope left for Jesus. But still!

In the end we told Holy Karl that he had to choose something that mattered especially to either Pretty Rosa or Jon-Johan.

"Okay," he said. "Then Pretty Rosa's going to cut Cinderella's throat."

He'd got us. Pretty Rosa couldn't bear the sight of blood, so separating Cinderella from her head was going to mean a great deal for her especially. Discussion over.

This time there were two who cried.

Pretty Rosa cried and begged for mercy and said she couldn't and that she'd just pass out in the middle of it all and maybe have an epileptic fit and have to be taken to the hospital and never be normal again. Elise cried like she'd never cried over her baby brother's coffin.

We didn't pay either of them any heed.

The first thing was for Pretty Rosa to pull herself together. Cinderella's head was a considerably smaller sacrifice than the ones many of the rest of us had been forced to make. The second thing was that we'd all suspected Elise had gotten off too lightly and had actually been happy about her brother's coffin being dug up. Holy Karl had found two sacrifices with one prayer.

Jon-Johan's father was a butcher and had a shop out front of the house where they lived. One early morning, after a couple of aborted attempts, Jon-Johan succeeded in sneaking away a long, newly sharpened carving knife that he took with him out to the sawmill and thrust into a wooden post, where it remained glinting and waiting for Pretty Rosa to pull herself together.

Which turned out to be sooner rather than later.

When we got to the sawmill a cold and stormy afternoon in the early autumn, Cinderella was no more; her head lay gaping resentfully at us on top of the heap, while her carcass lay draped across little Emil's coffin, that was now more red than crackled white.

White. Pink. Red is dead.

Pretty Rosa had looked oddly unmoved all day at school. Later she kept claiming she'd almost fainted and that it had been worse than horrifying and that she'd turned off the lights in the sawmill so as not to see the blood.

The thing about the lights had doubtless been for the better, because seeing the coffin now with all the blood and Cinderella's head without its body, Pretty Rosa passed out without a hint of warning. Huge Hans and Otto carried her over to the other end of the sawmill and piled up some boards to block the sight of both the coffin and Cinderella.

Taking her outside was out of the question in case anyone happened by.

Jon-Johan examined the knife, which had been stuck back into the post, now all begrimed with dried blood.

"Who would have thought Pretty Rosa had a butcher inside her!" he exclaimed, and laughed loudly.

He maybe wouldn't have laughed so much had he known what more Pretty Rosa could bring to pass.

XVI

There was something devious about it.

Not the matter of Pretty Rosa being able to cut Cinderella's throat without flinching and then just pass out at the mere sight of blood on the coffin, even if that was pretty odd in itself.

No, the deviousness became apparent when Pretty Rosa demanded the index finger of Jon-Johan's right hand.

It was a Tuesday afternoon shortly after we'd all arrived at the sawmill, drenched to the bone by an incessant, pouring rain that also found its way through the holes in the sawmill roof and made pools in the sawdust that we still weren't too old to paddle in.

Ursula-Marie said that was something that couldn't be asked for, especially not when it was Jon-Johan who played guitar and sang Beatles songs so it sounded almost like them, and he wouldn't be able to any more without his finger and so Pretty Rosa couldn't ask for it.

"Yes, I can," said Pretty Rosa, without explaining why.

"No, you can't," said Ursula-Marie, and the rest of us backed her up; a line had to be drawn somewhere.

"Yes, I can," said Pretty Rosa.

"No, you can't," we all said again.

And then, when it had all gone on long enough, it was like there was no strength left in Pretty Rosa, and our refusal was met by a weary silence that made us think we'd won.

At least until Sofie chipped in:

"What? Like Jon-Johan's finger doesn't matter?"

On that point we obviously couldn't disagree with her, but a finger was still something you couldn't just ask someone to hand over. But Sofie persisted and couldn't see why there should be any discussion.

"Everyone else has got what they wanted. And if Pretty Rosa wants Jon-Johan's finger, then she should have Jon-Johan's finger."

Eventually we agreed, since no-one was going to be able to bring themselves to cut off Jon-Johan's finger anyway.

"I will," said Sofie matter-of-factly.

We stared at her, mute, every one of us.

Something cold had come over Sofie ever since the thing about the innocence.

Cold. Colder. Frost, ice, and snow.

All of a sudden I remembered that Jon-Johan had been there that evening at the sawmill, and I didn't want to start imagining what he'd used his finger to do. But now I knew who had separated poor Cinderella's head from her body.

Sofie was a sly one.

I didn't tell anyone what I was thinking. Firstly, because I wasn't sure the finger didn't match up rather well with what Sofie had been made to deliver. And secondly, because I wasn't comfortable anymore with the thought of what else Sofie might be capable of.

I wasn't alone in feeling relieved that the heap of meaning was almost done.

Jon-Johan couldn't care less. For all he cared, it could have been the beginning or the end of the heap; there was no way he was giving up his index finger.

If Jon-Johan hadn't been the last of us, we might have let him off. For who could know what might be next? Or perhaps that isn't quite true. The truth is more likely that if Jon-Johan hadn't been the class leader, who decided everything and played guitar and sang Beatles songs whenever he felt like it, we would have let him off. As it was, there was no way out.

It would happen on Saturday afternoon.

First Sofie would cut off the finger, then we'd quickly apply a makeshift bandage, and then Holy Karl would run Jon-Johan home to Jon-Johan's parents in his trailer so Jon-Johan's parents could get him to the emergency room where he could be bandaged up properly.

On Sunday we were going to go fetch Pierre Anthon.

XVII

We spent Friday afternoon getting the sawmill straightened up.

It was December 14. There weren't many days until Christmas, but we weren't thinking about it. We had more important things to do.

We'd been hanging out at the old sawmill for more than four months and it showed. The sawdust was trodden up with dirt, candy wrappers and other garbage, and was no longer spread evenly over the concrete floor, but formed hills and peaks between pieces of lumber we'd dumped around the place for playing off-ground tag and sitting on. The spiders didn't seem to have reduced their activity on account of our presence. Rather, it was as if we'd increased their chances of a haul, and there were cobwebs in every nook and cranny. The windows, those that were still intact, were if possible even grimier than when we'd started.

After some arguing about who was to do what, we finally got going.

Frederik and Holy Karl picked up candy wrappers. Sebastian, Otto and Huge Hans gathered all the lumber at the back of the mill. And Maiken, Elise and Gerda clambered around brushing away cobwebs. Lady William, Laura, Anna-Li and Henrik Butter-up washed as much dirt off the windows as would come away, while Dennis knocked out the remainder of the broken window panes so there were no longer any jagged fragments to spoil the view out. Ursula-Marie and I took turns to rake the sawdust out neat using a rake we'd borrowed from Sofie. The old sawmill ended up looking almost decent.

One thing, though, we could do nothing about: the heap of meaning had started to smell less than pleasant.

Less than pleasant. Unpleasant. Sickening.

Part of it was down to Cinderella's etceteras on

and around Jesus on the Rosewood Cross, and part of it was down to the flies that were now swarming around Cinderella's head and carcass. An extremely unpleasant odour issued too from the coffin with little Emil inside.

It made me think of something Pierre Anthon had said some days before.

"A bad smell is as good as a good smell!" He hadn't any plums to throw at us and instead he slapped the palm of his hand against the branch he was sitting on, like he was accompanying his words. "What smells is decay. But when something starts decaying it's on its way to becoming a part of something new. And the new that's created smells good. So it makes no difference whether something smells good or bad, it's all just a part of life's eternal round dance."

I hadn't answered him, and neither had Ursula-Marie or Maiken who I was walking with. We just ducked our heads ever so slightly and hurried on to school without mentioning what Pierre Anthon had yelled.

Now I was standing here in the straightened-up sawmill holding my nose in the sudden knowledge that Pierre Anthon was right: something that smelled good would soon be something that smelled bad. And something that smelled bad was itself on its way to becoming something that smelled good. But I also knew that I preferred things to smell good rather than bad. What I didn't know was how I was ever going to be able to explain it to Pierre Anthon!

It was high time we got done with the meaning.

Time! High time! Very last call!

It wasn't as much fun as it had been either.

Certainly not for Jon-Johan.

He was whining already on the Friday while we were clearing up, and Otto telling him to shut up didn't help.

"I'll snitch," Jon-Johan replied.

Everything went quiet.

"You're not going to snitch," Sofie said coldly, but Jon-Johan was having none of it.

"I'll snitch," he repeated. "I'll snitch! I'll snitch! I'll snitch!" he kept saying, like a song with no tune.

Jon-Johan was going to snitch and say that the

story we'd worked out for him to tell his parents was all lies. That it wasn't true at all that he'd just found his father's missing knife and happened to cut his finger off when he yanked the knife out of the wooden post it had been stuck in.

All his whining was more than anyone could stand, so Otto yelled that Jon-Johan could shut his trap or else get beaten up. Not even that helped. So Otto was forced to beat up Jon-Johan, but that just turned his whining into a loud bawling, until Richard and Dennis took hold of Otto and said enough was enough. So we sent Jon-Johan off home and told him to come back the next day at one o'clock.

"If you don't turn up we'll beat you up all over again!" Otto hollered after him.

"No," said Sofie, shaking her head. "If you don't turn up we're going to take the whole hand."

We glanced around at each other. None of us was in any doubt that Sofie meant what she was saying. Not least Jon-Johan. He bowed his head and ran as fast as he could down the road and away from the sawmill.

———

Saturday, at ten minutes before one, Jon-Johan came back.

This time he wasn't running. He came walking, slowly, staggering almost, in the direction of the sawmill. I know because Otto and I were standing at the end of the road waiting, shivering in an icy wind with our hands buried deep in our pockets. Ready to go fetch him if he didn't show up of his own accord.

Jon-Johan began whining as soon as he saw us. I recalled Sofie's thin-lipped silence back then with the innocence and told Jon-Johan to shut his mouth and pull himself together. Cry-baby!

Cry-baby! Scaredy-cat! Jane-Johanna!

It didn't help.

Jon-Johan's whining only got worse when we got back to the sawmill and he saw the knife sticking up out of the plank that had been laid across the saw-horses where his finger was going to be *guillotined*. It was lady William who had provided us with this magnificent word for what was going to happen. Jon-Johan couldn't care less. He was howling absurdly at the top of his voice, and it was impossible

JANNE TELLER

to understand the sounds that were stopping short of becoming words in his mouth. One thing we did comprehend, though:

"Mum, Mum!" he wailed. "Mummy!" Jon-Johan threw himself down into the sawdust and rolled around with his hands in between his legs, and it hadn't even started yet.

It was pathetic.

Crybaby! Scaredy-cat! Jane-Johanna!

No, it was worse than pathetic, because Jon-Johan was the class leader and could play guitar and sing Beatles songs, but all of a sudden he'd become a howling little baby you just wanted to kick. One Jon-Johan had become another Jon-Johan, and we didn't care for this one. I thought maybe it had been this one Sofie had seen that night with the innocence, except that time it had been him on top, and suddenly I got shivers down my spine thinking about how many different people one and the same person can be.

Strong and feeble. Noble and mean. Brave and cowardly.

There was no fathoming it.

"It's one o'clock," Sofie announced, interrupting my train of thought. Probably just as well, because I no longer felt sure where we were headed.

Jon-Johan let out a long wailing sound and started rolling around in the sawdust with no thought for Ursula-Marie and me having raked it all so neat.

"Elise, Rosa, and Frederik, go outside and keep watch, and make sure no-one comes close enough to hear anything," Sofie continued, unmoved.

The door closed behind the three of them, and Sofie turned to Otto and Huge Hans.

"Now it's your turn."

Jon-Johan leapt to his feet and threw his arms around a post, and Otto and Huge Hans had to work hard to make him let go again. And then Richard and Holy Karl had to help drag him away with him thrashing about so.

"Ugh, he's pissing himself!" Richard exclaimed suddenly, and it was true.

Gerda giggled. The rest of us watched in disgust as a dark, uneven stream appeared in the sawdust.

Jon-Johan was still twisting and writhing when they got him over to the sawhorses. Huge Hans had to sit right down on top of his stomach. That helped, but Jon-Johan's fists were still clenched and he was refusing to open them despite the rather convincing physical arguments put forward by Otto and Huge Hans.

"If you don't put your finger on the block, we're just going to have to cut it off where you are," said Sofie calmly.

There was something eerie about how calm she was. Nevertheless, it was like it was rubbing off on the rest of us. What was to happen was a necessary sacrifice in our struggle for the meaning. We all had to do our bit. We had done ours. Now it was Jon-Johan's turn.

It's not like it was that bad.

When Jon-Johan again let out a loud wail, Hussain lifted up his arm that had just had its plaster cast removed and said:

"There's nothing to be afraid of. It's only a finger."

"Right, it's not going to kill you," said Huge Hans from on top of Jon-Johan's stomach and forced Jon-Johan's right hand to open.

"And if it didn't hurt," Anna-Li added quietly, "there wouldn't be any meaning in it."

_____

The knife grated deep into Jon-Johan's finger with a suddenness that made me gasp. I looked up at my green wedge sandals and took a deep breath. For a second everything was quiet. Then Jon-Johan screamed louder than I'd ever heard anyone scream before. I covered my ears, and still it was unbearable.

Four times Sofie had to go at it with the knife; with Jon-Johan thrashing around so much she had a job getting a clean cut. The third and fourth times I watched. It was actually quite fascinating to see how the finger turned into threads and stumps of bone. Then everything was blood, and it was just as well Pretty Rosa had been sent outside because there was lots of it.

It took an age, and then it was over.

Sofie slowly got to her feet, wiped the knife with a handful of sawdust, and then thrust it into the post like before. She wiped her hands on her jeans.

"That's that," she said, and went back to look for the finger.

Lady William and Maiken applied a rudimentary dressing to Jon-Johan's hand, Holy Karl brought his trailer forward, and when Jon-Johan's legs collapsed beneath him, Huge Hans carried him out and put him into it.

Jon-Johan was sobbing so much he could hardly breathe, and there was a large, brown, evil-smelling stain at the seat of his trousers.

"Remember, it's your turn to decide next!" Otto shouted to cheer him up, even though there was no-one left to be next.

Unless he was thinking about Pierre-Anthon.

Holy Karl got his pedals going, and the trailer drew briskly away with the whimpering Jon-Johan.

XVIII

I don't know what would have happened if Jon-Johan hadn't told on us. What did happen was that the police turned up at the sawmill before we even had any chance to get Pierre Anthon out there.

We were still there when they came. All of us.

What they later wrote to our parents was that besides twenty seemingly unmoved fourteen- and fifteen-year olds, they had found a foul-smelling heap of strange and macabre content, including the severed head of a dog, a child's coffin, possibly with contents (so as not to interfere with evidence, the coffin hadn't yet been opened), a bloody index finger, a desecrated Jesus statue, the Dannebrog, a snake preserved in formaldehyde, a prayer mat, a pair of crutches, a neon yellow bicycle, etc.

It was the etc. we found insulting. Like they could reduce the meaning to etc.

Et cetera. And so on. And more of the same that needn't be mentioned by name, at least not at the present moment.

We had no chance to object. What a commotion there was.

No-one saw any reason to take into consideration the fact that it was only eight days before Christmas.

Most of us were grounded, some were given a sound beating, and Hussain was again sent to the hospital where Jon-Johan had also been admitted. They were the lucky ones, they got to share a room and talk. The only thing I could do was lie in bed and stare at the wall and the striped wallpaper right from when the police took me home and gave the letter to my mother on Saturday afternoon until I was allowed to go to school on Monday morning with orders to come straight home. And that was only the start.

At school we got hauled over again.

We were hard and unyielding. Or rather, almost unyielding: a few started crying and saying they were sorry. Henrik Butter-up started sobbing and said it was all the rest of us who were to blame and that he had never wanted to be a part of any of it. Especially not the business about the snake in formaldehyde.

"Forgive me. Forgive me," Holy Karl wailed, so we all started feeling bad, so much that Otto eventually had to pinch him hard on the thigh.

"I'm sorry, I'll never do it again," whimpered Frederik and held his back so straight in his chair that it looked like he was standing to attention. At least until Maiken thrust the sharp end of a pair of compasses into his side.

Sofie looked scornfully from one renegade to the next. She herself was completely calm. And when Eskildsen after having bawled us out for thirty-eight minutes solid hammered his fist into his desk and demanded to know the meaning of it all, it was she who replied.

"Meaning." She nodded, as if to herself. "None of you has taught us any. So now we've found it ourselves."

Sofie was sent up to the Principal right away.

Rumour had it she simply repeated the same words to the Principal, even if he did give her a detention and bawl her out so it could be heard all the way down in the schoolyard.

When Sofie came back to class again there was a strange light in her eyes. I studied her for a long time. Apart from a slight blush at the top of her cheeks by the edge of her hairline her face was pale and unflinching, maybe with a touch of coldness, but also with a touch of fire for something. Without knowing exactly what, I knew that the fire was something that had to do with the meaning. I decided I wasn't going to forget it, no matter what happened. No matter that the fire wasn't something that could be added to the heap, or that I was ever going to be able to explain in any way to Pierre Anthon.

———

At break we stamped around, discussing what we were going to do.

It was cold, our hats and gloves were no use after only a short while, and the tarmac in the schoolyard was covered by a thin layer of slush that made our boots wet and unpleasant on our feet. But we had no choice; part of our punishment was that we were no longer allowed to spend recess indoors.

Some thought we should tell the whole story and make it clear that it was all Pierre Anthon's fault and then return everything to where it came from.

"Then they might let me raise the flag again," Frederik said hopefully.

"And I could go to church," added Holy Karl.

"Maybe it would be the best thing to do." Sebastian looked like he was already looking forward to going fishing again.

"No!" exclaimed Anna-Li, surprising us once again. "If we do that, then none of this has mattered one bit!"

"And nothing's going to bring Oscarlittle back,

is it?" Gerda added angrily, and she was right. Oscarlittle had succumbed to the first night of frost on December 3.

"Poor Cinderella," Elise sighed at the thought of the dog having died in vain.

I said nothing. It was mid-winter, and there was no good to be had of green wedge sandals at this time of year.

So far most of us were sticking together. There was full support for Sofie when she spat at the ground in front of Holy Karl's blue boots.

"Scaredy-cats!" she hissed. "Are you really going to give in that easily?"

Frederik and Holy Karl scraped coyly at the tarmac with their heels. Sebastian shrank some.

"It's just that we're in so much trouble, and we did do things we're not supposed to," Frederik ventured cautiously.

"Isn't that the meaning we've got out there at the sawmill?" Sofie looked Frederik straight in the eye and stared until he lowered his gaze and nodded. "If we give up the meaning, all we have is squat."

Squat! Zilch! Nothing!

"Are we agreed?" She looked around at the rest of us, more afire than ever before. "Isn't the meaning more important than anything else?"

"Of course it is," Otto said, and took the opportunity of giving Frederik a hard shove, so hard he almost made him fall.

The rest of us nodded and mumbled our agreement. Sure it was, of course, and it could be any other way. For that was how it was.

"There's only one problem left," Sofie continued. "How are we going to show Pierre Anthon the heap of meaning?"

She didn't have to explain what she was thinking. The police had cordoned off the sawmill and the heap of meaning to protect the evidence. And we were all grounded.

The bell sounded, and we were unable to discuss matters further until the next recess.

It was Sofie herself who provided the solution to the first part of the problem.

"With a bit of luck we can get round the cordon," she said. "There's a skylight at the side of the building facing away from the road and the entrance.

The police aren't guarding there. If we can get hold of a ladder we can get in that way."

Being grounded was trickier. Few of us felt inclined to challenge the wrath of our parents right now.

"Perhaps we could ask Pierre Anthon to go out to the sawmill alone and take a look for himself," Richard suggested.

"He'd never do it," Maiken said. "He'd think we were out to trick him."

I had an idea.

"What if *Tæring Tuesday* ran a story about us and the heap? Then he'd be sure to get curious and go out there himself."

"How are we supposed to get them to run a story about us?" Otto sneered. "The police are keeping it all secret because of our names and our age."

"We call the paper ourselves and pretend we're outraged townsfolk who've heard about the desecrated Jesus, et cetera." I chuckled at the thought.

"Just don't say et cetera when you call them!" Gerda shouted, no doubt thinking about Oscarlittle lying all stiff in his cage in the middle of the heap.

"I'm not going to make the call!"

"Who else?"

We looked at one another. I've no idea why they all ended up looking at me, but I guess that's what comes of not keeping your mouth shut.

Keeping your mouth shut. Keeping locked. Don't say _____.

I could have swallowed my tongue.

That afternoon I wasn't alone in the house for even a moment. The same again the following day. But the third day was perfect: my brother was at football, and my mum was going out to the store. No sooner had she cycled out of the driveway than I made straight for the telephone in the kitchen and pushed the number.

"*Tæring Tuesday*," said a sharp female voice.

"I'd like to speak to the editor, please," I said, mostly because I didn't know who else to ask for. I'd put a blouse over the receiver. It wasn't enough.

"Who should I say is calling?" asked the female voice, rather too inquisitively.

"Hedda Huld Hansen." It was the only name I could think of in a hurry, even if I did regret it right away since this was supposed to be anonymous. Still, it wasn't my name but the wife of the priest's, so why should I care. At least now I was being put through to the editor.

"Søborg speaking," he announced in a deep, resonant voice.

The voice was a comfort. It sounded kind and gentle like my granddaddy's, so I gave it the whole hog.

"Hedda Huld Hansen here. I'd like you to treat this in the utmost confidence, but I do believe it to be a matter *Tæring Tuesday* ought to take up." I drew my breath heavily, as if something was preying on my mind. "I'm sure you've heard about some of these dreadful goings-on at the church. First there was the business of the vandalism at the churchyard, with two gravestones being stolen, and then there was our very own Jesus on the Rosewood Cross being taken from the church, and on a Sunday at that." Again I took a sharp breath, making a hollow, rushing sound. "What I am certain you do not know, however, is that these national treasures have now been recovered. Together with the coffin of a small child, what's more, with contents, who knows, and a snake in formaldehyde, and a neon yellow bicycle, and," I lowered my voice, "a dog with its poor throat cut, and a dead hamster, a bloody index finger, and much more besides. Including a pair of green sandals." I couldn't help mentioning the sandals, even though it probably wasn't wise. Fortunately the editor didn't pay it any mind.

"How very appalling."

"Indeed. Shocking, don't you think? Out at the disused sawmill. And they say there's a group of children who have been collecting all these, what are we to call them, objects, with the idea of finding meaning. Indeed, there's supposed to be some kind of heap of meaning out there!" Again, I drew breath sharply through my teeth, almost whistling.

The editor repeated his view that this certainly was an appalling matter, but unfortunately he had no-one to put on the story at the moment, what with Christmas coming up. Before concluding the conversation, however, he made sure that the disused sawmill Hedda Huld Hansen was referring to was the one on Tæring Markvej on the outskirts of the town.

I think he believed it was all just a made-up tale, but still I hoped it had made him curious enough to put a journalist onto it. To be on the safe side I called Sofie. It was perhaps a good idea to keep a lookout for anyone coming by the sawmill.

There was a Christmas party at school (which we were excluded from attending), then came the day before Christmas Eve (and now our parents' hearts finally started to thaw), then it was Christmas Eve itself (and happily we were able to ascertain that we got just as many gifts as our more well-behaved brothers and sisters, and just as many as we'd received in previous years). But true Christmas arrived only on the day before New Year's Eve when *Tæring Tuesday* ran a story about demons having found their way to Tæring.

The demons were us.

Page three carried an exhaustive description of the heap of meaning.

Because our names weren't allowed to be made public, we weren't mentioned specifically, it just said that one of the senior classes at Tæring School was suspected of being involved. We were more than a little proud of ourselves, even if Pierre Anthon still hadn't shown up at the sawmill. When school started again on January 4 we paraded around the schoolyard, pulling ourselves up to full height and looking all superior so that the other pupils in our year and the junior classes too could be left in no doubt that we knew something they didn't. Several tried pumping us, but the only thing we were willing to reveal was that we had found the meaning.

It was Sofie who instructed us. We could mention the meaning and nothing else, so that was what we did.

"We've found the meaning!"

And that was what we told the teachers and the parents and the police and everyone else who kept on asking why.

And it was what we told the big press when they showed up.

XIX

The local newspapers came first. Then the popular dailies. Then the press from the capital and all the various regionals. Finally came the gossip weeklies and the local TV channel.

They were divided.

The first lot agreed with *Tæring Tuesday*: we were a bunch of rabble-rousers, way out of hand, who ought to be in reform school. The second lot, much to our astonishment, started going on about art and the meaning of life, while the last lot were mostly inclined toward the first. It wasn't long before the discussion for and against gathered amazing speed.

For! Against! For x Against!

We were stunned by it all, by the rage and the fury in their words, both for and against, and the fact that people from all over the country, but especially from the capital – even though they'd never before shown any sort of interest in Tæring and its environs – were suddenly arriving here in droves. One thing was certain: all the rage and the fury and the words for and against meant that the heap of meaning at once grew irresistibly more meaningful. But more important was that with all the press coverage and all these art critics showing up, and a whole load of other grand people, as well as a few ordinary ones, the police were forced to open up the sawmill and allow access on a daily basis between noon and four o'clock.

Now there was nothing to stop Pierre Anthon coming to see the heap of meaning.

What we hadn't bargained on was that Pierre
Anthon wouldn't.

"Nothing matters, and nothing's worth caring about. And that includes your pile of junk," was all he had to say.

And that was all he was saying no matter what we did. There was just no reasoning. Whether we tried coaxing or threatening, the answer was one and the same: No!

That disappointed us a lot.

In fact, it disappointed us so much that we almost lost heart because it rendered everything – Oscarlittle and the innocence and Cinderella and Jon-Johan's finger and little Emil and the Dannebrog and Ursula-Marie's blue hair and everything else in the heap of meaning – completely meaningless. And it didn't help in the slightest that more and more people were beginning to think that the heap was indeed meaningful, or that we no longer were frowned upon so much, neither by our parents, our teachers or the police.

We tried and tried again.

One at a time, in groups and the whole class at once (apart from Holy Karl who had been sentenced to do voluntary work for the church and was grounded four weeks longer than the rest of us). There was nothing we could do. It didn't even help when first the Swedish, then the Norwegian, then the rest of the Scandinavian and most of the European, and then the American and then at last what looked like the entire world press descended on Tæring and turned us all into something.

And something was the same as someone.

Regardless of what Pierre Anthon said!

It had been exciting when *Tæring Tuesday* wrote the story about us. It had been fantastic when the national dailies showed up and started quarreling about the heap of meaning. But it was quite beyond belief, and so very, very meaningful indeed, when the press suddenly began descending on Tæring from all corners of the world. Normally things were slow in Tæring in January. This year, January couldn't last long enough.

January.

January.

January.

January.

And January ran into February and the Shrovetide festival too, and when we got round to March 1 it was still January.

We were photographed head-on, from behind and from all sides, from above and below, and from all angles. The photographers chased us around to get the best smile, the most intelligent wrinkle of the brow, the most telling gesture. We were inundated with journalists ringing our doorbells, and TV-stations from all kinds of countries setting their cameras up outside Tæring School and filming us whenever we arrived or left. Even Jon-Johan was pleased and held up his stumpy bandage for all the photographers to see, so the missing index finger could be immortalised both here and there.

But above all the journalists and photographers were assailing the disused sawmill in order to find their own individual angles on the phenomenon.

The heap of meaning was soon renowned.

Everyone was impressed.

Everyone except Pierre Anthon.

XX

"It's all been seen before!" Pierre Anthon hollered, a cloud of frosty white breath issuing from the mouth of his dark blue balaclava. "It's news now, and the eyes of the world are on Tæring. In a month's time Tæring will be forgotten and the world will be someplace else." Pierre Anthon spat contemptuously at the sidewalk, but didn't get anyone.

Neither with his spit nor his words.

"Oh, shut up!" Jon-Johan yelled back at him haughtily. "You're just jealous, that's all."

"You're just jealous! You're just jealous!" the rest of us chanted in a triumphant echo.

We were famous, and nothing could bring us down.

Nothing could bring us down, because we were famous.

It was the day after the first British newspaper had shown up, and we weren't bothered one way or the other if Pierre Anthon didn't want to be part of the meaning and the renown. We couldn't have cared less. Not even about him not wanting to come out to the old sawmill to see the heap of meaning.

Couldn't, didn't, wouldn't care less.

And we couldn't have cared less about those who were against us and the meaning of the heap of meaning, either in Tæring or in the press, or any-where else in the country or even the world. For there were more and more who were for us. And so many people couldn't possibly be wrong.

Many! More! The truth!

The truth was made no less true by our being invited to Atlanta to take part in a television show that could be seen by everyone in the USA and the rest of the world too.

Everyone in Tæring was involved in the discussion about whether we should be allowed to go to America or not. Those citizens of Tæring who were against the heap of meaning and our own new-found significance, didn't even need to consider. No way should we be allowed to travel abroad and make fools of ourselves—and Tæring, and them, too, for that matter—in front of the whole world. As if things weren't bad enough already! The rest of the people in Tæring were proud of the invitation and of us and of the meaning, for Tæring had never before been accorded so much attention on any ac-count, no matter what the context.

Those in favour of the meaning were in the ma-jority.

Yet we were still banned from going.

The more people were in favour, the more reason there was to take extra good care of us and the heap of meaning. And whatever the people from the TV station said, no-one could be sure what might hap-pen to us over there on the other side of the Atlantic.

We were sad about that. But not that sad. People feeling they had to watch over us only added to our significance. So we thought.

Until we came by Tæringvej 25 again.

It was Monday morning, dark, cold and windy, and not especially pleasant to be on the way to school if it hadn't been for the meaning still overshadowing Maths and Danish and German and History and Biology and everything else that was tedious about Tæring. I was together with Ursula-Marie, Gerda and lady William, and as we leaned into the wind we were discussing whether or not we were significant enough for the hostess on the TV show in America to come to Tæring, now that we wouldn't be going to America to go on the show.

Lady William was quite certain.

"*Bien sur!*" he said, nodding his head. "*Bien sur*, she'll be here."

I thought it was a sure thing too, but before we got to discussing where the best place in Tæring would be to record the show, and what we were going to wear, we were interrupted by Pierre Anthon.

"Ha!" he spluttered, easily making himself heard above the wind from up there on the branch

of his tree. "As if not being allowed to go has anything to do with your safety! Ha, ha!" he laughed
emphatically. "How much money do you think
Tæring would get out of it if you went over there to
visit those journalists and photographers instead of
them coming here and staying at the inn and every-
where else where there's a vacant room to let, and
eating as well, and buying beer and chocolate and
cigarettes, and having their shoes mended and all
that kind of stuff. Ha, ha! How dumb can you get?"
Pierre Anthon swung his balaclava in the wind so it
became part of his laughter.

"He who laughs last, laughs longest!" Ursula-
Marie shouted. "Just you wait. If the meaning can't
go to the TV show, the TV show's bound to come to
the meaning!"

"True, indeed," Pierre Anthon laughed. "He who
laughs last, laughs longest!" And then he laughed
so loud it sounded like a whole bunch of incisive
arguments and conviction.

Ha, ha! Ho, ho! I'm right!

———

Whether Pierre Anthon knew what he was talking about or was just guessing, it turned out he was right.

We never did appear on television in front of the USA and the rest of the world, for even though we were now important and so very significant, the hostess on the show was even more important and even more significant. And she didn't have the time to come to Tæring and talk with us here.

That in itself was bad enough.

What was worse was that it planted inside me an unpleasant nagging suspicion that Pierre Anthon maybe had a hold of something: that the meaning was relative and therefore without meaning.

I didn't tell anyone about my doubts.

I was afraid of Sofie, but it wasn't just that. It was nice inside of the fame and the belief in the meaning, and I didn't want out of it, because beyond that there was only the outside and nothing. So I carried on parading myself around and looking superior, exactly as if I really had found the meaning and had no doubts whatsoever.

It was easy enough to pretend. To be sure, there were still a lot of people against us, but the very intensity of the fight over the meaning of the heap of meaning could only indicate that the matter was of the greatest significance. And significance was the same as meaning, and the greatest significance was therefore the same as the greatest meaning.

And I only doubted a tiny little bit.

Tiny little. Smaller. Nothing.

We won the struggle for the meaning, both at home and in the world's press.

The strange thing was that our victory ended up feeling like a defeat.

XXI

It was a big museum in New York that settled matters. It was referred to by an odd abbreviation that
sounded like something a child couldn't pronounce
properly. But however silly its name sounded, it
put a stop to the whole furious debate once and for
all when it bid three and a half million dollars for
the heap of meaning.

Suddenly everyone knew that the heap of meaning was art, and that only an uninitiated ignora-
mus could say otherwise. Even the art critic from
the biggest of the local newspapers backtracked
and said that he'd now considered the heap more
closely and that it was indeed a work of near-ge-
nius, comprising what perhaps was a quite novel

and original interpretation of life's meaning. He had only seen the work from the front the first time, he wrote.

Three and a half million dollars sounded like a fair amount of money, we thought, without really being able to grasp how much it actually was. Through the lawyer who had been hired to represent us we nevertheless insisted that the heap of meaning cost three million six hundred thousand dollars, on the basis that you should never sell anything cheaper than what you can get for it. Indeed, we actually ended up asking three million six hundred and twenty thousand dollars so there'd also be enough to pay the church for Jesus on the Rosewood Cross, who was no longer in a fit state to be returned anywhere.

The museum accepted, and the deal was closed.

The only thing remaining was to agree a date for when the heap of meaning would be collected.

To be sure, there were a lot of papers and permissions and other stuff to be dealt with before the heap could be moved across national boundaries. But at the same time—despite an unusually cold spring—

the perishable parts of the heap were perishing rather more rapidly for every day that passed. The museum eventually decided on April 8, four and a half weeks from the day. Then the museum people and their lawyers left Tæring, and with them the world's press, including our own national dailies. Tæring was once again exactly the same as Tæring always had been:

Dull. Duller. Dullest.

It was highly odd.

We had found the meaning and thereby the meaning behind everything. All kinds of experts had declared how magnificent the heap of meaning was. An American museum was paying millions of dollars for it. And yet no-one thought it was interesting any more. We were dumbfounded.

Either the heap was the meaning or else it was not. And since everyone had agreed that it was, it couldn't just stop being it again. Or could it?

We walked to and from school, but there wasn't a single camera, not a single journalist. We went out to the old sawmill. The heap of meaning hadn't changed (it wasn't in any way obvious that little Emil's remains had been removed from the coffin with its cracked paintwork and transferred to a new one that had then been interred and now was getting all cracked just like the first). Nothing was any different, and the fact that the heap looked smaller was probably nothing more than an optical illusion. Right?

A fact it was, however, that January and all our notoriety and the significance that came with it disappeared all at once in the first week of March.

Pierre Anthon was having a ball.

"Meaning is meaning. So if you really had found the meaning, you'd still have it. And the world's press would still be here trying to figure out what it was you'd found. But they're not, so whatever it was you found, it wasn't the meaning, because the meaning doesn't exist!"

We tried ignoring him and stuck our noses in the air and were superior and both something and someone.

At first we were doing so well we almost believed in it ourselves. It helped some to reread all the newspaper cuttings in the scrapbook and watch all the TV interviews from all the various countries that our parents had recorded on videotape. After a while, though, it was like all the cuttings began to fade, the interviews became tired comedies, and Pierre Anthon was having the game all to himself.

Doubt took us out one by one.

One. Two. All but one.

It was treason, and we weren't letting on to one another. But it could be seen in the way our smiles disappeared and were replaced by a mask that looked exactly like the one the grown-ups wore, which revealed all too clearly that maybe there wasn't that much that truly mattered.

Sofie was the only one of us to stick it out. And eventually it was her pale face alone and her burning eyes that kept the rest of us from giving up.

And admitting that Pierre Anthon was right.

XXII

It was spring, but this year spring couldn't reach us.

We were almost in our next school year and it wouldn't be long before we'd be having to choose new schools and new subjects. How on earth we were going to manage that with Pierre Anthon reminding us that nothing meant anything, we had no idea. Soon we'd be scattered to the four winds, losing contact with the meaning we had found and lost again without exactly knowing how it had all happened.

As though to reassure us that it wasn't yet spring at all, March kept sending afterblasts of winter. Late snow fell and melted, fell and melted. And once more again, the snow fell and melted, this time faster. Eranthis and snowdrops hid away, closed and frozen beneath all the white, and then when the final layer was gone for good, they pushed themselves up to signal renewal and spring flush among the few blades of grass that had stayed the winter out in Tæring.

In our class we saw neither renewal nor spring flush.

What was spring when fall soon would come around again, and all that now was germinating simply was to wither and die? How were we to find joy in the beech woods bursting into leaf, the starlings returning home, or the sun being higher in the sky for every new day that passed? All of it would soon be turning, running back the other way until it was cold and dark and there were no flowers and no leaves left on the trees. Spring was nothing but a reminder to us that we too would soon be gone.

Each time I lifted an arm was a reminder of how soon it would be lowered and turn into nothing. Each time I smiled and laughed it struck me how often the same mouth, the same eyes, were to cry until one day they would close, and others would go on laughing and crying until they too were put to rest beneath the soil. Only the course of the planets through the sky was eternal, and then only until Pierre Anthon one morning started hollering about how the universe was contracting and that one day it was going to collapse completely like a Big Bang in reverse. Everything would become so small and so compact as to amount to almost nothing. Not even the planets bore thinking about. And that's how it was with everything. It was all unbearable.

Bearable. Bearing up. All things, everything, nothing.

We were going around like we didn't exist.

Each day was like the next. And even though we looked forward all week to the weekend, the weekend was always still a disappointment, and then it was Monday again and everything started over, and that was how life was, and there was nothing else. We began to understand what Pierre Anthon meant. And we began to understand why the grown-ups looked the way they did.

And although we'd sworn we'd never become like them, that was exactly what was happening. We weren't even fifteen yet.

Thirteen, fourteen, adult. Dead.

———

Only Sofie still yelled back at Pierre Anthon whenever we walked by Tæringvej 25 and the crooked plum tree.

"The future's all here!" Pierre Anthon shouted, and waved his hand as if to show us that everything had been done and nothing was left for us but Tæring and the meaninglessness of it all.

The rest of us bowed our heads. But not Sofie.

"The future is what we make of it," she yelled back.

"Stuff and nonsense!" Pierre Anthon hollered. "There's nothing to make anything of, because there's nothing that matters!"

"There's a whole lot that matters!" Furious, Sofie hurled a handful of stones in the direction of Pierre Anthon. Some of them hit home, though not hard enough to bother him. "Come out to the sawmill, then you'll see what matters!"

I realized that Sofie really meant what she said.

For her, the heap of meaning was the meaning. Or maybe it would be more true to say that the heap of meaning meant something to her that it no longer did to the rest of us.

"Your junk doesn't mean a thing! If it did, the world's press would still be here and all the world's population would be flocking to Tæring to get in on the meaning."

"You won't see the heap of meaning because you haven't got the guts!" Sofie yelled as loud as she could.

"If your pile of garbage meant the slightest little thing, then there'd be nothing I'd rather do," Pierre Anthon replied condescendingly.

Then softly, almost pityingly, he added, "But it doesn't, or else you wouldn't have sold it, would you?"

For the first time since the innocence, I saw tears in Sofie's eyes.

She dried them away so angrily and so quickly with her fist that afterwards I wasn't sure I'd seen it. But she said nothing more to Pierre Anthon. And from then on she took another route to and from school.

There was just a week until April 8.

A week until the museum would pack, seal and dispatch the heap of meaning.

A week until Pierre Anthon was proved right for ever.

The rest of us had given up without a fight, but still the thought of Sofie giving up too was unbearable. And that was exactly what was happening. Or so I thought. But Sofie didn't give up. Sofie lost her mind.

XXIII

It happened suddenly, although thinking about it we realized it had been coming for some time. One minute Sofie was standing quiet and peaceable with the rest of us at the sawmill. The next minute she was running around banging her head against the posts and kicking sawdust up at the heap of meaning and wanting to climb up onto it and she would have pulled the whole thing apart had Otto and Huge Hans not taken hold and kept a tight grip on her.

It was the day before the museum people were coming to pack up the heap of meaning, and the meaning—or what was left of it—was for ever on its way out of Tæring.

"It's not their meaning, it's ours!" Sofie screamed, and only then did it occur to us that it was the first time in six days Sofie had said anything.

"We sold it to them!"

"But we can't sell the meaning!" Sofie hammered with her fists at Otto's chest and stomach, and I could see it was hurting him. Then Huge Hans got hold of her by the arms and twisted them behind her back, and now it was Sofie who was hurting.

I knew Sofie was right.

Meaning is not something you can sell. Either it's there or it isn't. Our having sold the heap of meaning had deprived it of its meaning. If there had ever been any. But I didn't wonder about that, because if it had never been there, then it wouldn't be Sofie but Pierre Anthon who was right.

"That's what we've done, and there's no more to be said!" Otto shouted back with such fury that I knew he too had realized that we shouldn't ever have done so.

"But then it means nothing!" Sofie yelled.

"Oh, come on, Sofie! Who cares about that heap?" Huge Hans shouted, and I found myself thinking that with the money from the museum he'd always be able to buy himself a new and better bike than his neon yellow racer. So what did he care?

"If the heap means nothing, then Pierre Anthon's right, and nothing matters!" Sofie went on. "Nothing!"

"Stop it, Sofie," Gerda yelled.

"Yeah, shut up, Sofie!" said Jon-Johan.

"Shut up, Sofie!" chimed in Elise, Hussain, Ursula-Marie, Holy Karl and a whole bunch of others, too.

But Sofie wasn't going to shut up. No way. Sofie started screaming even louder.

"Nothing," she screamed. "Nothing! Nothing! Nothing! Nothing! Nothing! ..."

Sofie screamed and screamed. She screamed so loud and so piercingly it made our ears ring and hurt right in to the bone. But the worst thing was that with that scream it was like everything fell apart. As though the heap of meaning truly no longer had any meaning, and with that all else lost its meaning, too.

Spring, summer, fall, winter, joy, sorrow, love, hate, birth, life, death.

It was all the same.

The same. One. Nothing.

It wasn't just me who understood.

And with that revelation it was like the Devil himself took a hold of us.

Hussain lashed out at Ursula-Marie for making him give up his prayer mat. Huge Hans kicked into Hussain and got back at him for the bike. Elise scratched at Otto and bit him as hard as she could, and then Ursula-Marie hit out at Elise, and Sofie laid into Huge Hans and tore at his hair until it came away in great tufts in her hands. Jon-Johan threw himself at Sofie and started punching away at her. Holy Karl joined him, since it was also Sofie who'd come up with the idea about Jesus and the rosewood cross. Frederik gave Maiken a slap in the face, and soon they were rolling around in the sawdust, but then Maiken wrestled herself free when lady William delivered Frederik a kick between the ribs. Maiken went for Gerda now, while lady William was floored by Anna-Li, just as Little Ingrid cracked Anna-Li over the head with one of her crutches, and Henrik grabbed the other one of Little Ingrid's crutches and thrust Little Ingrid onto the floor.

That was all I saw before Gerda jumped me from behind and I was pulled down, Gerda on top of me, and we tumbled around in the sawdust among all the others. Our fists hit home, untrained yet hard. I pulled at Gerda's hair and she at mine. Then she got hold of my earring and tore, and I screamed in pain. Her astonishment at suddenly sitting there with my earring in her hand allowed me to throw her off and leap to my feet. I brought my hand up to my ear and it was wet with sickly, warm blood. My eye caught sight only of more blood in the chaos of fighting bodies, blood that ran from the faces of my classmates and gradually was staining the sawdust and the concrete floor beneath.

It was like we wanted to kill each other.

And at once I knew I had to go get Pierre Anthon.

I managed to kick myself free of Gerda's grip

on my shins. I pushed my way through the ruck-us, disappeared out through the door, and ran off down the road.

I ran as hard as I could.

Ran like I'd never run before. I gasped for breath and got a stitch, and my throat and legs hurt, but I kept on running. I didn't know, what I was going to say to Pierre Anthon to make him come back with me to the sawmill. All I knew was that he had to come, that I had to, needed to, must get him back there.

Pierre Anthon was sitting on his branch in the plum tree staring emptily at nothing.

I could see his blue sweater from a distance among the light green of beginning buds. I ran until I reached the tree, then stopped dead on the pave-ment and at first could say not so much as a word, but could only cough and spit and gasp for the air that was all too reluctant to fill my lungs. Pierre Anthon considered my efforts in astonishment, and not without amusement.

"To what do we owe the honor, Agnes?" he said politely, though with a clearly mocking undertone.

I ignored his mockery.

"Sofie's gone crazy," I stammered as soon as I'd got enough breath back to speak. "They've all gone berserk. You have to come."

I was about to say more to try and persuade him, though I wasn't quite sure what. But Pierre Anthon slid from his branch without a word, hung for a moment from his arms, and then let himself drop to the grass below. He disappeared into the yard, only to appear again a moment later on his old gents bike and then sped off allowing me no chance at all to keep up.

By the time I got back to the sawmill, Pierre Anthon's bike was lying by the roadside where he'd let go of it and there was no sign of Pierre Anthon. The place was deathly silent.

I pushed open the door cautiously and went inside.

It was a gruesome sight that met my eyes.

Our class was standing in a semi-circle around Pierre Anthon.

Noses were beaten askew, eyebrows had been cut, teeth were missing, lips were gashed and swollen, eyes were red and bruised, an ear was all but torn away, and one or two looked like they could hardly keep themselves upright. All were smeared with blood and sawdust. But that wasn't what I saw. What I saw was the hatred.

Hatred. More hatred. All against all.

I pulled the door shut and edged my way along the wall into the sawmill.

Pierre Anthon's gaze went from one face to another.

"What a bunch of halfwits!" he exclaimed. He shook his head and moved slightly forwards. "If nothing matters, then there's nothing worth getting mad about! And if there's nothing worth getting mad about, then there's nothing worth fighting about either!" He looked around at each one of us, as though daring us to challenge him. "So what do you think you're doing?" He kicked at the sawdust and laughed derisively. "Is it that pile of junk you're fighting about?" He pointed with disdain, but then his attention was caught by something in it, though exactly what was hard to say.

Pierre Anthon stepped closer and walked slowly around the heap. He studied little Emil's coffin for a while with the rotting carcass of Cinderella on top. He considered Cinderella's head high up at the top of the heap, then allowed his gaze to move from the telescope to the Dannebrog, to the desecrated Jesus on the Rosewood Cross, the boxing gloves, the snake in formaldehyde, the six blue braids and the neon yellow bike, then on to the prayer mat and the crutches and to dead Oscarlittle and Jon-Johan's stiffened index finger. Then he caught sight of something that puzzled him.

"What's that rag?" he asked, pointing at the checked handkerchief.

"That's the meaning!" Sofie screamed hysterically. "That's the meaning!"

Pierre Anthon's eyes moved from Sofie to the rest of us. It was as though something was occurring to him.

"Oh, so that's the meaning!" he burst out angrily and grabbed hold of Sofie. He took her by the shoulders and sort of shook her until she stopped screaming. "And that's why you sold it?"

"The meaning," Sofie whispered.

"The meaning, ha!" Pierre Anthon scoffed. "If that pile of garbage ever meant anything at all, it stopped the day you sold it for money." He laughed again. He let go of Sofie and looked across at Gerda. "How much did Oscarlittle cost, Gerda, eh?"

Gerda didn't reply. Just blushed and looked down.

Pierre Anthon considered the flag for a moment, then turned his gaze to Frederik.

"King and Country!" he sneered. "You sold it all for filthy lucre, Frederik?" He shook his head. "I'm glad I'm not going to war with you as my general!"

Tears welled up in Frederik's eyes.

"And the prayer mat, Hussain? Don't you believe in Allah any more?" Pierre Anthon stared at Hussain who was standing with his head bowed. "What price was your faith?"

Pierre Anthon went on, naming the items in the

heap of meaning one by one, and one by one we writhed.

"And Jon-Johan, why not let your whole hand go, if you're willing to sell your finger to the highest bidder? And you, Sofie, what have you got left, now you've sold yourself?"

We didn't answer him.

Just stood scraping our feet in the sawdust, not daring to look, not at Pierre Anthon, not at one another.

"If it truly meant something, you wouldn't have sold it, would you?" Pierre Anthon concluded his tirade and threw his arm out wide in the direction of the heap of meaning.

Pierre Anthon had won.

But then he made a mistake.

He turned his back on us.

XXIV

Sofie was the first to lunge at him, and had the rest of us remained standing Pierre Anthon would easily have been able to shake her off. But we didn't. First followed Jon-Johan, then Hussain, then Frederik, then Elise, and then Gerda, Anna-Li, Holy Karl, Otto and Huge Hans, and then there was almost no room left for anyone else to kick and punch Pierre Anthon at the same time.

I don't know if it was gruesome or not.

Looking back on it now, it must have been very gruesome indeed. But that's not how I remember it. More that it was messy. And good. It made sense to beat up Pierre Anthon. It made sense to kick him. It was meaningful, even if he was down and unable to defend himself and eventually wasn't even trying.

It was he who had taken the heap of meaning from us, just as he had taken the meaning from us before that. It was his fault, all of it. That Jon-Johan had lost his right index finger, that Cinderella was dead, that Holy Karl had desecrated his Jesus, that Sofie had lost the innocence, that Hussain had lost his faith, that …

It was his fault that we had lost our zest for life and the future and were now at our wit's end about everything.

The only thing we were certain about was that it was Pierre Anthon's fault. And that we were going to pay him back.

I don't know what condition Pierre Anthon was in when we left the sawmill.

I do know what he looked like, although that wasn't what I told the police.

He was lying all awkward with his neck snapped back, his face all blue and swollen. Blood was running from his nose and mouth and had also colored the back of the hand with which he had tried to shield himself. His eyes were closed, but the left one was bulged out and seemed strangely askew beneath the gashed eyebrow. His right leg lay broken at a quite unnatural angle, and his left elbow pointed in the wrong direction.

It was quiet when we left, and we didn't say goodbye.

Neither to each other nor to Pierre Anthon.

That same night the disused sawmill burned to the ground.

XXV

The disused sawmill burned all through the night and still some the next morning.

Then it was over.

I arrived late in the morning. Most of the others were there already. We said hello, but didn't talk.

I considered what was left: the smouldering site of a fire.

It was impossible to tell what had been sawmill and what had been heap of meaning. Apart from the charred remains of walls, everything else was ash.

Gradually, the rest of them turned up, and soon

the whole class was assembled. No-one said anything. Not even to our parents, or the police or *Tæring Tuesday* or to the people from the museum in New York. The world's press hadn't shown; but if they had, I know we wouldn't have said anything to them either.

We didn't ask about Pierre Anthon, and it was a while before anyone connected his disappearance the previous day with the fire at the sawmill. It occurred to them only late that evening when his charred remains were found at the site of the fire. Close to what had once been the heap of meaning.

When the police got the idea that Pierre Anthon had set fire to the heap of meaning and the disused sawmill because he wouldn't accept that we'd found the meaning and were now famous, none of us was arguing. It was just sad that he'd become caught up in the flames himself.

We attended the funeral.

Some of us even cried.

Sincerely, I believe. And I should know, because

I was one of them. We lost the money from the museum, since no-one had thought of having the heap of meaning insured. But that wasn't why we cried. We cried because it was so sad and so beautiful with all those flowers, including the white roses from our class, because the shiny and unblistered white coffin, which was small despite being twice the size of little Emil Jensen's, shimmered and shone along with the light reflecting from Pierre Anthon's father's glasses, and because the music crept inside us and became greater and wanted out again without being able to. And it was so, whether we believed in the God we were singing for, or some other, or none at all.

We cried because we had lost something and gained something else. And because it hurt both losing and gaining. And because we knew what we had lost, but weren't as yet able to put into words what it was we had gained.

After Pierre Anthon's white and unblistered coffin had been lowered into the ground, after a gathering at the commune at Tæringvej 25, and after Mr. Eskildsen, Pierre Anthon's father and several people none of us recognised but guessed were Pierre Anthon's family had said a whole bunch of appreciative things about a Pierre Anthon none of us had known, we went out to the burned-out sawmill.

We somehow felt that it wouldn't be deemed appropriate for us to meet at the sawmill on this particular day, so for the first time in months we left three at a time by our four different routes.

The site was no longer smoldering.

All the embers were extinguished, only ash and charred rubble remained, cold and whitegrey-black. In the place where the heap of meaning had been, the ashes appeared slightly thicker, though it was hard to be sure. The place was littered with pieces of roofing and what was left of the pillars and beams. We helped one another straighten the place up. It was heavy, dirty work and we were black all over, even under our clothes.

We spoke as little as possible. Just indicated with a gesture and pointed when we needed someone to take hold of the other end of a beam or a stone.

In garbage cans close by we found empty bottles, plastic containers, and matchboxes, anything that could be used, and Sofie ran home and took what she could find, so that eventually there was a receptacle for each of us.

We used our hands to gather the ashes together.

The receptacles were carefully closed on the greyish mass that was all we had left of the meaning.

And we needed to keep a tight hold of it, for even though Pierre Anthon no longer sat hollering at us in his plum tree at Tæringvej 25, it still felt like we could hear him every time we passed by.

"The reason dying is so easy is because death has no meaning," he hollered. "And the reason death has no meaning is because life has no meaning. All the same, have fun!"

XXVI

That summer we were scattered to the bigger schools to the north, south, east and west, and Sofie was sent somewhere where they protect people like her from themselves.

We stopped playing together and never met again apart from by chance on the street where it couldn't be avoided. No-one has ever tried to bring us together for a class reunion or anything, and I doubt anyone would come if any of the teachers ever got the idea.

It's eight years ago now.

I still have the matchbox with the ashes from the

sawmill and the heap of meaning.

Once in a while I take it out and look at it. And when I carefully slide open the worn cardboard box and look into the grey ashes, I get this peculiar feeling in my stomach. And even if I can't explain what it is, I know there is a meaning.

And I know that the meaning is not something to fool around with.

Is it Pierre Anthon? Is it?

TRANSLATOR'S NOTE II

The children in the story are about fourteen years old, which puts them in seventh grade in Denmark, though in the United Kingdom or Ireland they would most likely be in Year 8/S2. Toward the end of the story, the children are dispersed to outlying schools. This is a common occurrence: small local schools in Denmark often provide schooling until the end of seventh grade only, at which point children move on to larger schools in larger communities.

JANNE TELLER was born to Austrian-German parents in Denmark, but since 1988 has lived in many countries around the world, such as Mozambique, Tanzania, and Italy. She has written several award-winning and bestselling novels, and her literature—including essays and short stories—has been translated into more than thirteen languages. Her novels for adults include the bestselling modern Nordic saga *Odin's Island*, *The Trampling Cat*, and *Come*.

Janne Teller has received numerous literary awards, and her controversial books repeatedly spark heated debate in Denmark and elsewhere.

Nothing won the prestigious Best Children's Book Prize from the Danish Cultural Ministry, as well as the esteemed Le Prix Libylit for the best novel for children published in all of the French-speaking world. In January 2011 it won the American Library Association's Michael L Pintzer prize and the Best Translation Award.

These days Janne Teller splits her time between Virginia and Copenhagen. Visit her website at janneteller.dk/?English.

Firebrand
ISBN 978-1-905537-19-8 (paperback, RRP £7.99)

It's the last decade of the sixteenth century: a time of religious wars in the full-mortal world. But the Sidhe are at peace, hidden behind the Veil that protects their world—until their queen, Kate NicNiven, determines to destroy it.

Seth MacGregor is the half-feral son of a Sidhe nobleman. When his father is assassinated, and Seth is exiled with his brother Conal to the full-mortal world, they vow not only to survive, but to return to reclaim their fortress and save the Veil.

But even the Veil's power can't protect the brothers when the brutal witch-hunts begin...

Brimming with intrigue and rebellion, *Firebrand* is the first book in the *Rebel Angels* series by Gillian Philip, the Carnegie Medal-nominated author of *Crossing the Line* and multi-award nominated *Bad Faith*.

Bloodstone
ISBN 978-1-905537-23-5 (paperback, RRP £7.99)

For centuries, Sithe warriors Seth and Conal MacGregor have hunted for the Bloodstone demanded by their Queen. Homesick, and determined to protect their clann, they have also made secret forays across the Veil. One of these illicit crossings has violent consequences that will devastate both their close family, and their entire clann.

In the Otherworld, Jed Cameron—a feral, full-mortal young thief—becomes entangled with the strange and dangerous Finn MacAngus and her shadowy uncles. When he is dragged into the world of the Sithe, it's nothing he can't handle—until time warps around him, and menacing forces reach out to threaten his infant brother.

In the collision of two worlds, war and tragedy are inevitable—especially when treachery comes from the most shocking of quarters...

Bad Faith
ISBN 978-1-905537-08-2 (paperback, RRP £6.99)

Life's easy for Cassandra. The privileged daughter of a rector, she's been protected from the extremist gangs who enforce the One Church's will.

Her boyfriend Ming is a bad influence, of course, with infidel parents who are constantly in trouble with the religious authorities. But Cass has no intention of letting their different backgrounds drive them apart.

Then they stumble across a corpse. What killed him? How did his body end up in their secret childhood haunt? And is this man's death connected to other, older murders?

As the political atmosphere grows feverish, Cass realises she and Ming face extreme danger.